YOU CHOOSE

AN INTERACTIVE SPORTS STORY

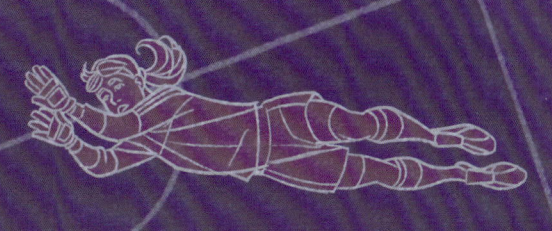

BY BRANDON TERRELL
ILLUSTRATED BY FRAN BUENO

CAPSTONE PRESS
a capstone imprint

You Choose Books are published by Capstone Press, an imprint of Capstone.
1710 Roe Crest Drive
North Mankato, Minnesota 56003
www.capstonepub.com

Copyright © 2021 by Capstone Press, a Capstone imprint. All rights reserved. No part of this publication may be reproduced in whole or in part, or stored in a retrieval system, or transmitted in any form or by any means, electronic, mechanical, photocopying, recording, or otherwise, without written permission of the publisher.

Library of Congress Cataloging-in-Publication Data
Names: Terrell, Brandon, 1978- author. | Bueno, Fran, illustrator.
Title: Game day soccer : an interactive sports story / by Brandon Terrell ; [illustrated by Fran Bueno].
Description: North Mankato, Minnesota : Capstone Press, [2021] | Series: You choose: Game day sports | Audience: Ages 8-11. | Audience: Grades 4-6. | Summary: Facing a mighty opponent on the soccer field, the reader's choices can mean the difference between a triumphant victory and a heartbreaking loss.
Identifiers: LCCN 2020039275 (print) | LCCN 2020039276 (ebook) | ISBN 9781496696076 (hardcover) | ISBN 9781496697097 (paperback) | ISBN 9781977154286 (ebook pdf)
Subjects: LCSH: Plot-your-own stories. | CYAC: Soccer--Fiction. | Plot-your-own stories.
Classification: LCC PZ7.T273 Gaq 2021 (print) | LCC PZ7.T273 (ebook) | DDC [Fic]--dc23
LC record available at https://lccn.loc.gov/2020039275
LC ebook record available at https://lccn.loc.gov/2020039276

Editorial Credits
Editor: Angie Kaelberer; Designer: Kayla Rossow; Media Researcher: Eric Gohl; Premedia Specialist: Katy LaVigne

Printed and bound in China. PO6238

TABLE OF CONTENTS

About Your Game 5

CHAPTER 1
New Team, Same Rival 7

CHAPTER 2
Striking on the Front Lines. 13

CHAPTER 3
Speedy Winger 39

CHAPTER 4
Turning up the Defensive Heat 71

CHAPTER 5
A Worldwide Sport 103

Glossary 106
Test Your Soccer Knowledge 107
Discussion Questions 110
Author Biography 111
Illustrator Biography 111

ABOUT YOUR GAME

YOU are a talented soccer player known for working hard and using your athletic ability and instincts to help your team win. But this is the beginning of a new season, and you're on a different team than in the past. And this new team just happens to be the top rival of your former team. Can you put your old loyalties aside to help lead your new team to victory?

Chapter 1 sets the scene. Then you choose which path to read. Follow the directions at the bottom of the page as you read. The decisions you make will change your outcome. After you finish one path, go back and read the others for new perspectives and more adventures.

CHAPTER 1
NEW TEAM, SAME RIVAL

"This just doesn't look right."

You're staring at yourself in the full-length mirror in your bedroom. Around it, the walls are cluttered with posters of your favorite pro soccer players. The rest of the room contains nothing more than an unmade bed and a bunch of cardboard boxes.

You shake your head. You can't believe the soccer jersey you're wearing. It has a black stripe down the middle and across the front is the word *Jaguars*.

You shake your head. "We had to go and move, didn't we?" you mutter.

Turn the page.

After your mom was recently promoted at work, your family moved to a bigger house in a new neighborhood. The only problem? You also had to switch schools.

And not to just any school. And not just at any time of year. No, you moved near the end of the soccer season to the school on the other side of the city. Your crosstown rivals. You went from being an East Bridgeton Badger—the elite soccer team in the city—to a West Bridgeton Jaguar, your fiercest rival. And today, the two teams face off in the playoffs.

The field at West Bridgeton Middle School is teeming with people when you show up. Everyone wants to see the teams battle it out. You just never thought you'd be on the other side of the battlefield.

As you get out of the car and sling your duffel bag over your shoulder, you can't help but put your head down. It feels like everyone's watching and whispering.

When you get to the bench, Coach Stevens is waiting. "Are you ready for the game of your life?" she asks.

You nod, but say nothing.

The rest of your teammates are lacing up their sneakers or dribbling soccer balls in the grass. Among them is Malia, the tallest player on the team. You also see Hannah, who has quick eyes and a killer bend in her kick. Jasmine, the team goalie, is there too.

They all look at you when you arrive. You know what their stares mean.

Turn the page.

You were an enemy. Worse, a Badger. And here you are, on their team. Playing in a game that will determine if the team moves on in the tournament.

You sit on the bench and lace up your sneakers in silence. The ref blows a whistle.

"All right, bring it in!" Coach Stevens yells. Your teammates start to gather their things. Quickly, you pull Coach Stevens aside.

"What's up?" she asks.

"I know I'm new," you reply, "and the rest of the team has played a whole season together. Plus," you nod across the field at the Badgers, "I used to be one of them. I just wanted you to know, as a way to show everyone I'm a team player, I'm cool playing any position on the field you want."

Coach Stevens nods. "I like that attitude," she says. "Where do *you* think you'd be best at playing?"

> To take the lead and be the team's striker, turn to page 13.
>
> To opt to play left forward, turn to page 39.
>
> To decide you're best defending the team at wingback, turn to page 71.

CHAPTER 2
STRIKING ON THE FRONT LINES

"The new girl's gonna play where?" Hannah asks incredulously.

"You heard me," Coach Stevens replies. "Striker. And you'll be her left wing."

You played striker for the Badgers, so when Coach Stevens asked you where you felt comfortable playing, the answer was obvious. At striker, you have the best chance to score and prove to your new team that you're on the field to win. After all, it is your old team and friends you're up against, and you know their moves better than anyone.

Turn the page.

But this was also the response you'd expected from your new teammates. They don't trust you yet.

"We're a team out there," Coach Stevens says sharply. "No matter what position we play."

The referee blows a whistle, signaling the teams to start the game. You can see the looks your teammates are giving each other. They don't agree with Coach Stevens's decision. And as they start to walk out onto the field, they already look deflated and defeated.

It's your job as striker to lead the team. But how can you do it if they don't trust you? You could show them your leadership on the field. Or you can stop the feeling of mistrust before the game by talking with them.

To pull the team aside now and talk to them, go to page 15.
To show them your leadership on the field, turn to page 34.

"Hey, everyone," you say. "Huddle up!"

The team looks over at you. They appear surprised. But they jog over, and you all cluster together.

"Look," you say. "I know it's weird having an ex-Badger as the center of the team. But we're here to win this game, and we can only do that together. I'm with you." You hold out your hand, palm down. "Are you with me?"

They glance at each other. Then Jasmine places her gloved hand on yours. Others follow. Hannah is last. "We are," they say.

"Then 'Go, Jaguars' on three," you reply. "One ... two ... three ..."

"GO, JAGUARS!"

The pep talk seems to work!

Turn the page.

As the game begins, you feel the energy as the Jaguars race up and down the field. But you can also sense the Badgers' aggressiveness. Especially in their striker, Zoe Moore.

"Watch out, traitor," Zoe says as you run down the field together. "I'm coming for you."

The ball soars in your direction, and you manage to stop it with your left foot. You zip past Zoe. You're on a breakaway, dribbling swiftly into your zone. The middle of the field is wide open. But so is Hannah to your right.

> To pass the ball to Hannah, go to page 17.
> To take the shot yourself, turn to page 21.

The Badger goalie is crouched, eyes focused on you. Hannah throws up her hand.

In one swift move, you hook the ball with your toe and rocket it over to Hannah. She thrusts out her chest and the ball hits her perfectly, landing at her feet. She dribbles upfield and unleashes a kick that bends high and right.

The Badger goalie is thrown off by your pass and can't recover. The ball sails into the net. The Jaguars have scored the first goal of the game!

As you jog back to midfield together, Hannah holds out her fist. "Nice assist, newbie," she says with a smirk.

"Thanks." You bump her fist back.

Hannah's goal is a huge boost for the Jaguars' confidence.

Turn the page.

Your other winger, Bao Khang, uses her mad ball-dribbling skills to carve her way down the field and score a second goal for the Jaguars. Your new team has skills, that's for sure.

But Zoe Moore is doing what she can to remind you of your past. "You used to play for the best," she taunts. "Now look at you."

"Look at the scoreboard, Zoe," you reply.

The ball is headed your way. A Badger defender races after the ball, but you think you have a chance at getting there first.

To let the Badger defender get the ball, go to page 19.
To go for the open ball, turn to page 28.

You slow down. A collision is the last thing you need.

The defender gets to the ball and dribbles it down the field. She passes it to Zoe, who dishes to a winger racing down the left side.

Turn the page.

It looks like she's going to get a shot on goal. From nowhere, the Jaguars' quick midfielder, Luna Barnes, is there to stand in her way.

Thwump!

Luna knocks the ball free, shattering the Badgers' chances.

The Badgers have a no-quit attitude, though. The next time they have the ball, their passing skills are on full display. Zoe bends a kick over Jasmine's outstretched hands.

"Goal!" the ref shouts. They've cut the lead to one.

It's nearly the end of the first half. Your teammates are getting tired. Hannah is sweating. Malia is sucking in air, hand on her cramped side. You know you need to do something to get your team back in the game.

Turn to page 30.

Yes, Hannah is open. But the middle of the field is right there in front of you! The chance to prove your worth to your new team is too tempting. So you dribble the ball upfield, ignoring Hannah's shouts and waves.

You flip the ball from one foot to the other, doing your best to deceive the Badger goalie, Mara Rinehart. But Mara knows you too well. She smirks as you line up and drill the ball at the goal.

Mara dives right, perfectly snagging your shot out of the air!

As she overhand tosses the ball back into play, you hear Malia behind you. "Ball hog," she mutters.

Turn the page.

The Jaguars are definitely not jelling as a team, and you feel like a monkey wrench in their well-oiled machine. A sloppy pass from Malia to Hannah is easily intercepted. Bao trips a Badger player accidentally and is called for a penalty. You're supposed to be leading the team, but you can't pull them together.

Steffi Powers, the Jaguars' other main defender, gets the ball. She boots it high into the air. It's sailing right toward you. But you aren't the only player nearby. You could try to jump up and header the ball. Or you could anticipate a pass and slip toward the goal.

> To back away from the incoming ball, go to page 23.
> To jump up and header the ball, turn to page 29.

You step back, keeping your eyes on the ball. It comes toward Malia, who had the same idea as you and jumps to header the ball.

It bounces off her forehead . . . right toward you!

You knock the pass down with the inside of your left foot, then dribble upfield. Mara is favoring the left side of the goal, so you fake her out and lace a shot at the upper-right corner of the net.

Swish!

"Great shot!" Malia concedes. Maybe her attitude toward you is changing.

The Badgers up their aggressiveness. Each time you and Zoe both go for the ball, you jostle into one another.

Turn the page.

In the second half, the Badgers even the score. The Jaguars are exhausted and in desperate need of a breather.

"Time-out!" Coach Stevens yells.

"All right, everyone," Coach Stevens says. "Stay calm. Don't play their games, and keep a level head. You've got this!"

The team members nod and take deep breaths. The time-out was just what you needed.

As the second half progresses, you see the Jaguars have regained some strength. When the Badgers have a breakaway and Zoe takes a great shot on goal, Jasmine is there to stop it.

Jasmine swings the ball out to Jaguar midfielder Luna Barnes, who passes to Malia. Malia sees you in the middle of the field and slips a great pass to you.

You see Bao up ahead. But this is also a great chance to score a goal.

> To pass to Bao, turn to page 26.
> To take the ball upfield yourself, turn to page 30.

You've got a wide-open lane in front of you now, but spy Zoe out of the corner of your eye. You decide it's best to pass the ball off to Bao.

The pass lands perfectly in front of her, leading Bao right toward the goal. Mara crouches, prepared. Bao sizes up the shot and lets it fly.

Thwack!

Mara dives in front of the ball, and it slaps off her gloved hands. She leaps up and snatches the ball before you can get to it and take a follow-up shot.

When the final buzzer sounds, the score is still tied. You're going to overtime!

Overtime is more of a struggle, and neither team is able to score.

"Okay, everyone!" Coach Stevens says. "Looks like we've got ourselves a shootout!"

In the shootout, five players from each team will take a free shot at the goal. The only question is where you'll fit in this new lineup of strong Jaguar players.

Coach Stevens answers the question for you. She points at you and says, "You're up first."

To agree with Coach Stevens and kick first, turn to page 32.
To tell her you'd prefer to kick last, turn to page 33.

The Badgers are playing fast and hard, so you decide you need to as well. You lower your head and race toward the ball.

You get there at the same time as the Badger defender, colliding with a loud smack. Her elbow slams into your ribs. You try to breathe, but the wind has been knocked out of you.

Your cleat gouges into the defender's ankle. Your own ankle twists, and another jolt of pain hits you. This time, you fall to the grass.

"Come on," Coach Stevens says as she helps you to your feet. "You need to sit down until we can get that ankle looked at."

You take a spot on the bench and watch in pain as the Badgers come back to win the game.

THE END

To follow another path, turn to page 11.
To learn more about soccer, turn to page 103.

It bothered you that Malia called you a ball hog. You want to prove her wrong. As the ball spins toward you, you leap up to hit it with your head and pass it to her.

There's just one problem. Malia had the same idea! She jumps up, and the two of you collide in midair. You both fall to the grass as a Badger slips in and takes the ball away.

"What were you thinking?" Malia shouts.

"I'm sorry," you say weakly.

At the other end of the field, the Badgers score. Malia and your other teammates look upset with you, and it shows on the field. You barely get the ball for the remainder of the game. And the Badgers run away with an easy victory.

THE END
To follow another path, turn to page 11.
To learn more about soccer, turn to page 103.

You take the ball upfield yourself. Zoe cuts you off, but you're able to slip past her. When you're close to the goal, you fake a pass to Hannah but take the shot yourself. It sizzles into the top corner of the net!

"Great shot!" Hannah and Malia say together. The team is invigorated by this goal, and you've done your job gaining their trust.

The Jaguars' confidence doesn't waver. Before long, Hannah has added another goal, stretching your lead.

There's not much time left on the clock, and the angry Badgers know it. They push and shove, struggling. You can't believe this was the style of game you used to play.

When good teamwork and solid passing lead to another goal by Malia, you smile. This new team? They're a great group to play alongside.

With the lead and a loud, packed crowd, you and the Jaguars easily hand the Badgers a solid defeat.

THE END
To follow another path, turn to page 11.
To learn more about soccer, turn to page 103.

You nod. "Yes, Coach," you say.

As the first Jaguar to kick, it's your job to set the bar for the team.

With a ball tucked under one arm, you stride onto the field. You set the ball down and prepare to kick.

You step back, eye the goal, and pick your spot. Then you race up and boot the ball with the inside of your right foot. It hooks left, curling toward the corner of the goal.

Mara dives. The ball strikes her forearms and falls. You missed!

Unfortunately, yours is not the only shot she blocks. By the time the shootout has ended, the Badgers have won by a shootout score of 3–1.

THE END

To follow another path, turn to page 11.
To learn more about soccer, turn to page 103.

You step back and hold up your hands. "I think someone else should go first, Coach," you say. "Set the bar and all."

"Fine," Coach Stevens says. "Hannah, you're up."

"Got it," Hannah replies. She grabs a ball and jogs onto the field.

You watch as Hannah confidently scores the first goal of the shootout. Bao follows with another, and Malia adds a third. The Badgers keep pace, though. So when it's your turn to kick last, the shootout score is tied.

You line up your shot. Mara looks unsure. You aim left, but fake her out and kick to the right. The ball sizzles past her. The Jaguars win!

THE END
To follow another path, turn to page 11.
To learn more about soccer, turn to page 103.

You see the looks passing between your teammates as you take the field to start the game. You get it. You're new, and you're taking the lead. How could this possibly go well?

You consider huddling up, giving them a pep talk. But it's better if you *show* your team that you are a leader.

The Badger striker, Zoe Moore, is waiting for you at midfield. She used to be your friend. Now she just smirks at you. "Good to see you," she says mockingly. She's trying to get under your skin. "Have a great game."

It's clear from the start that the Jaguars aren't jelling as a team. You attempt to pass the ball up to Hannah, but your aim is off and it sails past her, out-of-bounds.

"Come on, newbie!" Hannah shouts, slapping her hands together in frustration.

Turn the page.

You don't know what to do. You want to help your new team, but whatever you do, it seems to backfire. You feel like a failure.

This isn't me, you tell yourself. *I can do this. I can help the Jaguars win.* You take a deep breath and try to refocus on the game.

For a while, your efforts to calm yourself seem to help. Late in the first half, as you bring the ball up the field, you see Hannah and Bao are both struggling to get open. Hannah breaks free, but isn't looking your way. But it's the perfect chance to pass to her!

"Hannah!" you shout, kicking the ball in her direction.

Hannah glances over at you, but it's a second too late. As she lunges for the ball, she becomes tangled with a Badger defender. To your horror, they both fall to the ground in a heap.

Hannah moans in pain as Coach Stevens and the team rush to her side. As she passes you, Malia asks, "Did you do that on purpose?"

"What? No."

Her eyes say she doesn't believe you.

You can only watch as Hannah is helped off the field. Your team won't be following your lead now. And even worse, all the Jaguars seem to lose their confidence. It's no surprise to any of you when the Badgers win the game.

THE END
To follow another path, turn to page 11.
To learn more about soccer, turn to page 103.

CHAPTER 3
SPEEDY WINGER

You mull over Coach Stevens's question. "It's not my place to play striker," you say. "Not for my first game. But I'm fine playing forward. I'll take left wing, if that's cool."

"Done," Coach Stevens says. "Hannah, you're striker."

The Jaguars jog out onto the field. You're nervous about facing your old team, and you can see they're glaring at you. Especially Zoe Moore, the team's striker. "Be careful," you tell the other Jaguars. "The Badgers love to be aggressive and to get the other team penalized with yellow and red cards."

"Good to know," Hannah says.

Turn the page.

As the game starts, the Badgers are bumping and playing hard. Zoe shakes past Hannah, using her left hand to shove off where the referee won't notice.

"Hey!" Hannah shouts.

Moments later, it happens again. This time, Malia is knocked over while fighting for the ball. Again, the refs don't see what's happening.

You start to think that you'll need to play as aggressively as the Badgers to win the game. But should you?

> To play as aggressively as the Badgers, go to page 41.
> To continue playing Jaguar-style, turn to page 50.

If Zoe and the Badgers are going to play rough, then you're going to have to play at their level.

You race down the field. The Badger defender goes after the ball at the same time. You bump and nudge. Not enough to get called for a penalty, but enough to let the Badgers know you remember how you used to play.

Early in the game, Hannah and Zoe tangle for the ball. It breaks free and heads in Malia's direction.

Malia sees you and sends a skittering pass in your direction. The ball is in front of you, and you're not sure you'll be able to reach it. The defender races to your side, keeping pace. You're both trying desperately to reach the ball before it goes out-of-bounds.

> To let the ball go out-of-bounds, turn to page 42.
> To try to reach the ball and pass it, turn to page 45.

You know you won't reach the ball before it goes out-of-bounds. The Badger defender takes a swipe at it. Her toe hooks the ball but doesn't stop it.

"Jaguar ball!" the ref shouts.

You take the throw-in, holding the ball high over your head. Hannah dashes past a stumbling defender, and you hurl the ball at her.

Hannah deftly dribbles upfield. She spies Bao, the other Jaguar winger, across the way and passes it over.

Bao immediately shoots.

Swish!

The ball hits the back of the net! "Goal!" the ref shouts.

The Jaguars have the lead. And as the game continues, Malia is able to add a second goal.

This doesn't sit well with the Badgers. You can see the fire and intensity in their eyes. As Zoe takes the ball upfield, you spy Jaguar midfielder Luna Barnes rushing up to meet her. Zoe drops a shoulder, and Luna collides with her.

"Penalty!" the ref says, holding up a yellow card on Zoe.

"Oh, come on!" Zoe protests. "*She* ran into *me*."

Luna hobbles off the field. She's injured but should be able to make it back into the game.

The Jaguars get the ball back. After some fancy passing, Malia winds up with a breakaway. A Badger defender catches up to her, and the two tangle for the ball.

"Watch out!" you hear Malia shout.

Turn the page.

The Badger falls to the grass. This time it's your team that gets called for the penalty.

Things are starting to get out of control. You look to Coach Stevens, hoping she sees it too.

> To get your coach's attention to call a time-out, turn to page 55.
>
> To trust that the team will pull itself together, turn to page 57.

You're playing fast and hard and won't let the ball go out-of-bounds.

You race after it at the same time as the Badger defender. She gives you a light shove in the back.

"Oof!" you say as you stumble forward. Your right elbow strikes the defender in the chest, knocking her over. The ref blows the whistle.

Tweet! "Penalty, Jaguars," she calls, pointing at you.

The call is unfair, though. You feel like you need to plead your case with the ref.

To let the penalty slide, turn to page 46.
To plead your case with the referee, turn to page 59.

You open your mouth to protest the penalty, then immediately close it. No, arguing isn't the way to win this game.

The Badgers have a corner kick. As the ball comes into play, Zoe snags it but fails to score.

Time is running out, and the score is tied! Seconds are left on the clock. Zoe rockets a shot at goal, but Jasmine blocks it. She scoops up the ball and overheads it in your direction.

The Badgers have a strong line of defenders coming at you as you dribble the ball past midfield. You're very aware that time is ticking away.

Out of the corner of your eye, you see Bao. It's a long pass across the field to her, but she's more open than you.

You have a split second to decide.

> To make the risky pass to Bao, turn to page 48.
> To take the shot yourself, turn to page 61.

The Badgers in front of you mean business. Bao has a much better angle than you on the goal, even though she's across the field. It's a dangerous pass to make, but there are only seconds left on the clock. You need to decide *now*.

"Bao! Heads up!" You twist your body and uncork a pass that sails quickly across the field toward Bao. And she's ready for it.

But so are the Badgers.

A Badger defender peels off, racing to the ball and intercepting it from Bao.

Time expires before she can do anything, though. You're headed to overtime!

"I know you're tired," Coach Stevens says as you prepare for overtime. "But I have faith in you. Dig down deep and find that strength. Got it?"

"Yes, Coach!" the team shouts in unison.

The game has been grueling, and overtime is no different. It's a long, tiring battle. Your legs strain as you run down the field. They feel like jelly—as if you could fall over at any second.

For most of overtime, neither team gets any advantage. Jasmine and Mara, the two goalies, stop everything that comes their way.

But then, as Jasmine overheads a pass to Hannah, the ball bounces past the Jaguar striker. It skitters across the grass, right toward Zoe! Zoe meets it and dribbles effortlessly on a breakaway.

You race to catch up. You're the closest player to Zoe. She's near the goal and about to shoot. Jasmine looks tired, and you're not sure she'll be able to stop Zoe's shot this time.

> To trust Jasmine to make the save, turn to page 62.
> To try to block Zoe's kick yourself, turn to page 63.

You're used to the way the Badgers play—hard, aggressive, relentless. But that doesn't mean your new team has to play that way. They've got their own method, and you're a part of *their* team now. So you play that way too.

And it works. The team is jelling, and you're a big part of that. Your job as winger is to pass the ball and get your team in scoring position.

Hannah brings the ball up the field. As she does, you dash past the Badger defender, who's caught between following you and going after Hannah. This is the best chance you've had to score, and you want to give the Jaguars the early lead. You throw your hand up. "Over here!"

Hannah sees you and passes it over. But the pass is high, and you're not sure how to stop the ball.

To jump up and header the ball, go to page 51.
To use a forearm to knock down the ball, turn to page 53.

You leap into the air just as the ball reaches you.

Smack!

The ball bounces perfectly off the crown of your head. It sails over Zoe and a second Badger defender and lands in front of Bao, the other Jaguar winger.

Bao easily slips a shot past Mara Rinehart, the Badger goalie.

"Nice shot!" you say, bumping fists with Bao.

"Nice pass!" she replies.

The Jaguars hold the slim lead through the first half.

The second half remains a tight battle. Hannah manages to score, but so does Zoe. The Jaguars' lead is still one goal, and time is ticking away.

Turn the page.

With just moments left on the clock, the ball heads your way. It's flying high again, and you have a chance to do a difficult midair kick. The ball's location isn't ideal. If you nail it, though, you'll surprise the goalie and give the Jaguars a strong lead with almost no time for the Badgers to come back.

To let the ball land, turn to page 65.
To attempt the midair kick, turn to page 67.

You could try something that'll make the crowd roar, but that's not the smart play. Not in this situation. So instead you decide to use your forearm to stop the ball.

But as the ball reaches you, you realize you've mistimed it.

Thwack!

The ball strikes your gloved left palm.

The ref blows the whistle, and the ball goes back to the Badgers.

This move shifts the game's momentum in the Badgers' favor. Zoe is able to score near the end of the first half. In the second half, there's a flurry of goals. Soon you find yourself in a tie game.

Turn the page.

Less than a minute is left on the clock. Hannah brings the ball up the field. She sees you open on the left side and passes you the ball. You take it, dribbling toward the goal. The defender, who was guarding Malia, hurries your way. But you have a clear shot and a chance to break the tie game.

To aim for the left side of the goal, turn to page 68.
To aim for the right side of the goal, turn to page 69.

Things are getting away from you. If you're not careful, the Badgers will take over the game completely. You turn to the bench and signal Coach Stevens by making a *T* with your hands.

"Time-out!" she calls.

The team huddles together. They look tired and in pain.

"Catch your breath, everyone," Coach Stevens says. "Get some water. We've got this."

You nod. "Remember to play smart," you tell the team. "Don't fall for their tricks, and don't get too wild so you're called for a penalty."

The team nods in agreement.

When the ref blows the whistle and you all jog back out onto the field, you can already tell the time-out was worth it. Jasmine is standing a bit taller, and the pain in Hannah's side has gone away.

Turn the page.

The Jaguars look ready to play.

The Jaguars play a strong second period, not caving to the Badgers' intense play. The refs have also caught on to their tactics, as Zoe is called for a pair of penalties late in the game.

With minutes left on the clock, Hannah takes a high pass and performs a perfect header, knocking the ball past the goalie. Bao adds another goal late in the game, securing the victory for the Jaguars.

As the Badgers slump off the field, you and your new team celebrate a strong victory!

THE END
To follow another path, turn to page 11.
To learn more about soccer, turn to page 103.

It's OK, you think. *We've got this!*

Instead of asking Coach Stevens for a time-out, you gather the Jaguars. "We can do this!" you say, bumping fists with Bao.

The Badgers are relentless, though. As the second half starts, they score a quick flurry of goals, three in all. They've taken the lead!

It looks like the Jaguars are not used to the same level of intensity as the Badgers, and they're wearing down.

"Time-out!" Coach Stevens calls.

The team hurries to the sideline. Jasmine, the goalie, looks completely gassed. And she's not alone.

"I don't know how much more I've got," Hannah says, grabbing at her side. She's gulping in air.

Turn the page.

It's clear the Badgers have you right where they want you. As time trickles away, they score another goal past the tired Jasmine.

The Jaguars are now too far behind to come back. It looks like you'll have to wait until next season to beat the Badgers.

THE END

To follow another path, turn to page 11.
To learn more about soccer, turn to page 103.

"Come on, ref!" you say, running over to her. "There's no way I elbowed her on purpose!"

The ref just looks at you and says nothing.

"It's not fair and you know it!" You're letting your anger get the best of you. It doesn't help that Zoe is standing behind the ref with a sly smirk on her face.

Turn the page.

Bao hurries over. You think she's there to back you up. Instead, she stands between you and the ref.

"Hey," she says to you, "chill out."

Bao drags you away from the ref. You can feel your heart thudding against your rib cage. You got out of hand, and you'll have to deal with the consequences.

Coach Stevens glares at you as you reach the bench. "Arguing with the ref is *not* how we play," she says. "Find a spot on the bench and warm it. Your game is done."

You slump onto the bench. This wasn't how your first game as a Jaguar was supposed to go. You can only watch as the Badgers come back to dominate the game and win.

THE END
To follow another path, turn to page 11.
To learn more about soccer, turn to page 103.

Yes, your old teammates are coming up fast. They're in your face. But you find a gap and dribble through them.

It's just you and Mara Rinehart, the Badger goalie.

You unleash a bending shot that sails high. For a second, you're afraid it'll soar over the goal. But it catches the corner, just out of Mara's grasp.

You did it!

Time expires, and you and the Jaguars are victorious!

THE END
To follow another path, turn to page 11.
To learn more about soccer, turn to page 103.

Sure, Jasmine's tired. But you've come to trust your new teammate.

Zoe shoots, and sure enough, Jasmine snags the ball out of the air.

"Great save!" you shout.

Jasmine hurls the ball downfield, where a waiting Hannah takes it. She dribbles past a defender and takes her own shot.

Swish!

"Goal! Jaguars win!" the ref bellows.

The team races out onto the field. You've done it. You've beaten your old team and made a lasting memory with your new one.

THE END
To follow another path, turn to page 11.
To learn more about soccer, turn to page 103.

It's been a long game. Jasmine's tired. You can see it in her eyes. And you've got a chance to make sure the Badgers won't be able to score.

So you take it.

You speed up, catching Zoe as she reaches the front of the goal. However, as you go to kick the ball, your leg strikes her below the knee, knocking her to the grass.

"Penalty," the ref shouts.

Zoe stands, brushing herself off. You can't believe you made such a dumb mistake. And since it occurred in front of the goal, Zoe will have a free penalty kick.

Turn the page.

The ref drops the ball, and Zoe lines up for the penalty shot. She stutter-steps, fakes right, then kicks high and to the left.

The ball sails past Jasmine, right into the goal.

The game is over. The Badgers celebrate their overtime win as you sulk off the field in defeat.

THE END

To follow another path, turn to page 11.
To learn more about soccer, turn to page 103.

You decide the ball is too high for a successful midair kick. There's no way you're going to attempt a bad kick. You wait for the ball to land.

When it does, you notice you have a clear shot on goal. You take the shot.

Whoosh! The ball flies past Mara, hitting the back of the net.

You've extended the Jaguars' lead with little time left on the clock. The Badgers don't have enough time to catch up. Jaguars win the game! You're going to the championships!

THE END
To follow another path, turn to page 11.
To learn more about soccer, turn to page 103.

You leap into the air, swiveling your hips and kicking the ball. It's not perfect, though, and neither is your landing. As you come back down, your ankle twists in the grass.

"Ouch!" Pain jolts up your leg, and you crumple to the ground.

The team rallies around you, helping you limp off the field. When you reach the bench, Coach Stevens says, "Put some ice on that ankle. You need to sit out and rest it."

As you watch, the Badgers rally late, coming from behind to beat your new team.

THE END
To follow another path, turn to page 11.
To learn more about soccer, turn to page 103.

You're a right-footed kicker. And Mara, the goalie, knows that. So she'll be anticipating a kick to the right side of the goal.

So you aim left.

Mara is ready, though. She dives and snags the ball out of midair.

"I'm open!" Zoe shouts from the far side of the field.

Mara hurls the ball in her direction, and Zoe takes it upfield. She doesn't have the same bad luck as you, though. She sneaks a goal past Jasmine, breaking the tie.

As time runs out, the Badgers are victorious.

THE END
To follow another path, turn to page 11.
To learn more about soccer, turn to page 103.

Mara crouches. She's leaning slightly to the left, so you're aiming for the right side of the net.

Whump!

You kick the ball with the side of your foot, sending it to the right side of the goal. Mara, off-balance, tries to dive that way. But she comes up short, and the ball sails over her head.

You did it!

As time expires, the Jaguars win by your last-second goal. You helped your new team win, and you can't stop smiling.

THE END

To follow another path, turn to page 11.
To learn more about soccer, turn to page 103.

CHAPTER 4
TURNING UP THE DEFENSIVE HEAT

"So what'll it be?" Coach Stevens asks.

"I know how aggressively the Badgers play," you say. "So I'll play wingback and defend against them."

Coach Stevens nods. "All right," she says. "Hit the field, team!"

As you take the field, Jasmine sidles up next to you. "Glad you're back on 'D' with me," she says. "I remember last season, when you hooked that goal past me." She shakes her head. "I lost sleep over that shot. So I'm happy you're a Jaguar now."

Turn the page.

As the game begins, you notice the Badgers playing aggressively. Zoe Moore, their striker, is swift and relentless. Within the first few minutes of play, she finds a way to break past you and score a goal.

"How's the new team treating you?" she asks smugly. She used to be your friend. Apparently, that's changed. She's set on humiliating you and Steffi Powers, the other Jaguar defender.

Moments later, the Badgers have another breakaway. Zoe and her wingers are racing toward you. Steffi stumbles, and Luna Barnes, a Jaguar midfielder, is on the far side of the field. You have to decide who to attack.

> To focus your attention on Zoe, go to page 73.
> To anticipate Zoe passing the ball, turn to page 83.

Zoe is the team leader and the strongest Badger on the field. You race over to cover her.

But your haste in reaching Zoe is exactly what she wants. With fast footwork, she flips the ball to the open winger. The winger scores, and the Jaguars are quickly down 2–0.

Come on, you tell yourself. *You have to focus.*

As Zoe jogs back to midfield, she comes up behind you. "Hey, I don't remember you playing this terrible when you were a Badger!" You try to remain emotionless, but inside, you're fired up.

Just before the end of the first half, Hannah scores. This cuts the Badgers' lead to 2–1. The game is fast and intense, more than you thought it would be. By the time the first half ends, you're sucking in air and in need of a break.

Turn the page.

"Everyone in," Coach Stevens says. She waves you all over. "That was a wild first half. But we're still in this game. One goal is all it takes to shift the momentum. Are you ready to go out there and take this game back from them?"

"Yes, Coach!" the team bellows.

As you prepare to walk out onto the field, Coach Stevens stops you. "Have a seat," she says. "You need a few more minutes of rest."

> To plead with Coach to let you play, go to page 75.
> To start the second half on the bench, turn to page 79.

"Come on, Coach," you plead. "I'm good to go. Trust me."

Coach Stevens eyes you, then nods. "OK," she says.

As the second half starts, you feel good. Zoe tries to dribble the ball past you, but you block it and send the ball forward to Hannah in the middle of the field.

But just then you feel light-headed. The soccer field seems to be spinning around you.

You shake your head, and things come back into focus.

The ball comes skittering back toward you. You chase after it, but the dizzy feeling returns. You stumble and fall, sliding across the grass.

The ref stops play, and a sub hurries onto the field. "You!" She points at you. "You're out!"

Turn the page.

You can't blame Coach Stevens. You should have taken the extra time at the half.

As you sit on the bench, regaining your strength, Zoe slips another goal past Jasmine, increasing the Badgers' lead. Frustrated, you wait until Coach Stevens finally waves you back into the game.

There's little time left on the clock, though, and you're down a pair of goals.

Two Badgers race downfield, passing the ball back and forth. You've got your eyes on Zoe. It looks like she's about to pass the ball.

> To anticipate her pass, go to page 77.
> To stick with covering Zoe, turn to page 88.

You have played alongside Zoe before, so you know this move. But then, she's also aware of that fact.

You shift back, waiting for the pass as Steffi hustles over to help. And yes! Just as you expect, Zoe kicks the ball toward the winger. But you're right there to intercept it.

"Luna! Heads up!" You pass the ball over to her on the left side, and Luna brings it past midfield. You watch as she hits an open Malia. Malia sends the ball past the Badger goalie.

"Yes!" you shout, pumping your fist.

Momentum has shifted back in the Jaguars' favor. You can feel the energy as the team huddles together before the game restarts. But there isn't much time left on the clock, and you're still down a goal.

Turn the page.

The two teams battle back and forth, neither getting a clear shot on goal. You look up at the clock. Less than a minute left.

"Time-out!" Coach Stevens calls. It's your last one. She says something to the ref, who nods. "Jasmine!" She waves the goalie to the sidelines.

She's pulling the goalie!

That leaves an empty net but also gives the Jaguars one more player on offense.

To ask Coach Stevens to play offense, turn to page 89.
To decide to stay on defense, turn to page 90.

Coach Stevens is right. You could use the extra rest.

You start the second half on the bench, watching as the Badgers score again, putting them ahead by two goals. Then Hannah finds a way to slip past Zoe, sending a kick high into the upper-right corner of the net.

Swish!

"All right," Coach Stevens says, waving for you. "You're back in. Go get 'em!"

You hurry back onto the field.

The shift in momentum has Zoe flustered. And when she's flustered, she gets physical. And mouthy. "We're better off without you," she says. "Just look at us dominating you."

"Game's not over yet," you fire back.

Moments later, the Badger right winger races past midfield with the ball. She passes up to Zoe, who dribbles toward the goal. You rush over to meet her.

"Behind you!" Steffi calls out. But your focus is on Zoe. You're determined to stop her.

To heed Steffi's warning, go to page 81.
To ignore Steffi and continue toward Zoe, turn to page 93.

Zoe is your focus. But you can't ignore Steffi's warning. She literally has your back.

You glance over your shoulder. A second Badger is racing up behind you. You skid to a stop, your cleats catching in the grass. The Badger brushes past you, narrowly missing a collision.

As you stop, Zoe passes the ball. You twist your body toward it and lash out a leg.

Thump.

You intercept the pass, hearing Zoe draw in her breath sharply. You pass the ball to Luna, who sends it past midfield.

The pass hits Malia, and the Jaguars send the ball around, confusing and confounding the Badger defenders until Hannah is able to sneak a goal past Mara.

Turn the page.

She's tied up the game! You glance up at the clock. There's just over a minute left!

The Badgers get the ball. Their defender kicks it high and wide, and it sails past midfield like an incoming rocket. It's arcing down right at you! From the corner of your eye, you see Zoe coming toward you.

> To wait for the ball to come down, turn to page 94.
> To jump up to header the ball, turn to page 95.

You see Steffi stumble, and Luna is too far away. You know that Zoe is the Badgers' best player, but that doesn't mean you should ignore the other offensive players on the field. You slide to your right to defend against the pass.

Zoe sees this too and takes the shot herself.

Jasmine shuffles left, and the ball lands squarely in her waiting arms. It's a sweet save, and it reminds you that if you're going to win, you'll have to trust your new teammates.

The Jaguars score a pair of goals in the first half, taking the lead. But that doesn't sit well with the Badgers. They were playing aggressively at the start of the game. Now they're being downright brutal.

The right winger sweeps for the ball and takes out Steffi at the legs.

Turn the page.

Tweep! The ref calls a penalty.

Zoe shoves Luna from behind.

Tweep! Another penalty.

It's getting rough.

Zoe brings the ball down the field. While you want to be as aggressive as she is, you know it's better to hang back. She goes to pass the ball, and you see the other Badger is wide open.

> To stick with covering Zoe, go to page 85.
> To turn and play for the pass, turn to page 96.

Keep your eyes on Zoe, you tell yourself.

She passes the ball, just as you expected. And you're there to intercept it. The ball flips into the air. You jump up and kick it with all your strength past midfield.

Turn the page.

Malia takes the ball and tries to score, but the Badgers goalie blocks her shot. At the end of the first half, your team has a one-goal lead.

But the Badgers aren't giving up without a fight. The second half is rough and relentless. They aren't backing down or giving up any more goals, which makes your job as a defender that much harder.

After a great save by Mara Rinehart, the Badger goalie, your opponents bring the ball up the field. Zoe leads the way, taking a pass from the left winger. She's got a clear shot at the goal.

You race over. There's a chance you can stop her. But should you take it?

> To let Zoe go free toward the goal, go to page 87.
> To try to intercept Zoe, turn to page 97.

Zoe is about to shoot. She draws her foot back.

You consider diving in front of the ball, but that's risky. So you let Jasmine take the shot. Unfortunately, Zoe is too good. The Badger striker slips it past Jasmine to tie up the game!

The two teams battle through overtime, neither getting the advantage over the other. When time expires, the score is still tied.

"It's a shootout," Coach Stevens says.

"Let me go first," Hannah offers.

This may be your time to shine, though. You consider asking Coach Stevens if you can go first.

But should you?

> To suggest that you kick first, turn to page 98.
> To let Hannah kick first, turn to page 100.

You're no newbie—you played alongside Zoe and know this move. She's going to fake a pass and take the shot herself.

You race up to her . . .

And she boots the ball to the other Badger!

You've misjudged the play, and the winger easily scores. The Badgers' lead is strong, and there's little time left. You've basically just handed them the win.

"Looks like it's game over," Zoe says.

And sadly, she's right.

THE END
To follow another path, turn to page 11.
To learn more about soccer, turn to page 103.

Do you want to play offense and make the game-tying goal? You bet you do.

"I'll be the extra player!" you offer.

Coach Stevens nods in agreement.

The Jaguars have a corner kick. Malia takes it, sending the ball high and in your direction. This is it! You leap up to header the ball toward the goal—but a Badger defender does the same thing! She beats you to it, knocking the ball away. Zoe scoops it up and delivers a cross-field kick that sails into the open net just as the clock expires.

It's game over, and the Jaguars have lost. You wish you had kept playing defense. Maybe the outcome would have been different.

THE END

To follow another path, turn to page 11.
To learn more about soccer, turn to page 103.

You'd love to play offense. But that open goal behind you is scary. So you opt to stay on defense.

And it's a good thing too. As Malia takes a corner kick, a Badger deflects it with her head. The ball lands near Zoe, who boots it toward the open goal.

Just before it slides past the goal, you race over and intercept the shot. You quickly pass forward to Luna, who sends it to Bao past midfield.

Seconds remain. Time is running out!

Bao hurries up the field. You watch nervously. "Come on," you whisper.

Bao passes to Hannah, and just as time expires, Hannah sends a shot that sails past the Badger goalie. You're tied!

Turn the page.

In overtime, the momentum is clearly in the Jaguars' favor. Jasmine is back on the field. After a stellar stop, she overheads the ball past midfield to Malia.

Malia bends a kick that the Badger goalie was not expecting.

Swish!

It strikes the back of the net.

"Jaguars win!" the ref shouts.

You join your team at midfield to celebrate your amazing, come-from-behind victory!

THE END
To follow another path, turn to page 11.
To learn more about soccer, turn to page 103.

Steffi is shouting, but you barely hear her. Zoe is your primary focus.

As you reach her, though, the Badger left winger comes up behind you. You barely see her before she collides with you. You tangle limbs, and you both fall hard to the grass.

Pain ripples through your ankle. It's twisted.

"Let me help you," Steffi says. She takes your hand, and you try to stand. But applying too much pressure is agonizing.

You should have listened to Steffi. Because you didn't, the Badgers end up with the win, and your season is likely over due to injury.

THE END
To follow another path, turn to page 11.
To learn more about soccer, turn to page 103.

In this situation, a header is dangerous. You're not going to risk it.

Zoe doesn't think that way, though. As the ball comes down, she leaps up and hits it squarely with her chest. The ball rolls harmlessly away as time expires.

In overtime, the Badgers get the ball on a breakaway. Zoe fools Jasmine and sends the game-winning shot past the Jaguar goalie.

The Badgers have won, and you can only watch as they celebrate on the field.

THE END

To follow another path, turn to page 11.
To learn more about soccer, turn to page 103.

Zoe isn't going to back down, and neither will you. It's a risky move, but you jump into the air.

Whump!

The ball strikes you on the crown of your head, sailing past Zoe and right to Bao!

Bao takes the ball upfield. Seconds remain.

She shoots and scores!

The crowd goes wild! The Jaguars have won on a last-second shot! And your risky move was crucial in the victory!

THE END

To follow another path, turn to page 11.
To learn more about soccer, turn to page 103.

Zoe is going to pass. You've been her teammate, so you know her moves. And so you turn to face the other Badger.

Zoe does pass the ball. But as she does, she bumps into you. You stumble forward, bracing your fall with your hands.

As you hit the grass, your left wrist tweaks. Pain shoots up your arm and into your fingertips.

You jog to the sidelines, clutching your injured wrist.

"Looks like you're sitting this one out," Coach Stevens says. She hands you an ice pack.

You can only watch as the Badgers come back and win.

THE END

To follow another path, turn to page 11.
To learn more about soccer, turn to page 103.

Zoe is about to shoot. You see her draw her foot back.

There isn't much time. You dive feetfirst, sliding across the grass in front of her.

The kick sails forward and strikes you right in the nose. You feel a wave of pain, and your vision blurs as your eyes water.

While you're down, the Badger winger takes a shot. And since Jasmine is distracted by you, the ball sails past her.

Coach Stevens comes to help you off the field. Your nose is throbbing. "It's not broken," she says, "but you'll have to come out."

You sit on the sidelines, waiting for the pain to stop, as the Badgers beat your new team.

THE END
To follow another path, turn to page 11.
To learn more about soccer, turn to page 103.

"I can take the first shot, Coach," you say before Hannah can ask again.

Coach Stevens looks at Hannah. Hannah nods. "It's her old team," she says. "Makes sense."

Coach Stevens agrees. "Now let's go out there and win."

You're the first of five Jaguars to shoot a kick on goal. Mara crouches and stretches as you place the ball and line up your shot.

Thwack!

You send it sailing to her left, but Mara dives, deflecting the ball and denying your kick!

You see Zoe smirking. "Nice try," she mouths to you.

This wasn't the plan. And it only gets worse. The Badgers score three shootout goals, and the Jaguars only manage two. You've lost the game.

THE END

To follow another path, turn to page 11.
To learn more about soccer, turn to page 103.

You'd like to take the first shot. But you're new to the team, and Hannah is their leader.

"Show us the way, Hannah," you say, bumping fists with her.

Hannah does just that! She sneaks the first goal past Mara.

When it's your turn, you line up like you're going to do the opposite of Hannah. But then you do the same thing. You score!

The Jaguars wind up making four of the five shootout goals. Jasmine saves three of the five Badger kicks, sealing your victory!

THE END
To follow another path, turn to page 11.
To learn more about soccer, turn to page 103.

CHAPTER 5
A WORLDWIDE SPORT

Soccer is one of the world's oldest sports. Its history dates to a game played with a ball more than 2,000 years ago in China. By the 1100s, the game had spread to England. It involved kicking a ball, but wasn't much like today's game.

Today, two teams of 11 players compete on a field with goal nets at each end. One player from each team, called a goalkeeper, guards each net. The players on the field use their feet, torsos, and even their heads to pass the ball down the field. They try to get the ball into the opposing team's net and score a goal. Only the goalkeepers are allowed to touch the ball with their hands.

The version of soccer we know began in England in 1863. Several English soccer teams united and formed the Football Association (FA). In much of the world, soccer is called association football or just football.

As the sport developed, rules were added. The FA was an amateur league, meaning the players weren't paid. That changed in the late 1800s, as England and other countries created professional leagues. By 1900, soccer was being played around the world.

The Fédération Internationale de Football Association (FIFA) formed in 1904. FIFA oversees the sport on a global level. In 1908, soccer was officially included in the Olympic Games. FIFA hosted the first World Cup, soccer's championship competition, in 1930. In 1996, women's soccer became part of the Olympics.

Soccer is the most well-known sport internationally. In the 1990s, its popularity began to grow in the United States, thanks in part to its hosting of the 1994 FIFA World Cup.

Today, Major League Soccer (MLS), the professional men's league in North America, has 26 teams. Three are in Canada and the rest are in the United States. The LA Galaxy is the most successful MLS team, with five MLS Cup titles.

The National Women's Soccer League formed in 2012, and as of 2020 it had nine professional women's teams. On an international level, the U.S. Women's National Soccer Team has had great success. The team has won four gold medals and one silver medal in the Olympics and four World Cup championships, the last in 2019.

GLOSSARY

breakaway (BRAY-kuh-way)—when one or more attacker gets behind the defender, so that only the other team's goalkeeper is between them and the goal

card (KARD)—a signal of a penalty by a player; yellow cards are given as a caution to a player, while red cards mean the player must leave the field

forward (FOR-wurd)—a player who plays nearest to the opponent's goal net; also called a winger

header (HED-ur)—using the head to pass, shoot, block, or otherwise control the ball

midfielder (MID-feel-dur)—a player generally positioned on the field between the defenders and forwards

shootout (SHOOT-owt)—a method used to break ties after overtime, when teams alternate taking penalty kicks

striker (STRY-kuhr)—a forward whose main job is to score goals

throw-in (THROH-in)—a play that occurs when the ball goes out-of-bounds; the opposing team of the team who last touched the ball is allowed to throw the ball onto the field

wingback (WING-bak)—a player who plays in a wide position on the field, taking part both in attack and defense

TEST YOUR SOCCER KNOWLEDGE

1. Who is the only player on the field allowed to touch the ball with his or her hands?

   A. striker

   B. goalie

   C. forward

2. How many people play at one time on a soccer team?

   A. 10

   B. 9

   C. 11

3. What is another name for soccer?

   A. association football

   B. foot game

   C. affiliated goals

4. What is soccer's international championship called?
- **A.** World Series
- **B.** Football Championship
- **C.** World Cup

5. How is a soccer game started?
- **A.** tip-off
- **B.** throw-in
- **C.** kickoff

6. What are the field players who play closest to the opposing net called?
- **A.** forwards
- **B.** midfielders
- **C.** wingbacks

7. What piece of equipment are players required to wear in an organized game of soccer?
- **A.** mouth guard
- **B.** shin guards
- **C.** gloves

8. Which throw-in would be considered improper?

A. the player jumps while throwing the ball

B. the player throwing the ball uses both hands

C. the player throwing the ball tosses it from over his or her head

9. What is the box around the goal called?

A. goal box

B. hands-free zone

C. penalty box

10. If an offensive player is fouled inside the penalty box, the result is a _____.

A. corner kick

B. penalty kick

C. direct kick

Answers: 1. B 2. C 3. A 4. C 5. C 6. A 7. B 8. A 9. C 10. B

DISCUSSION QUESTIONS

- ▶▶▶ Describe a time when you joined a new team or played against a team with your friends on it. How did it feel?

- ▶▶▶ You are writing an article for the school's website about the Jaguars. Choose one outcome and describe it from your perspective. Did the Jaguars win or lose?

- ▶▶▶ What is your favorite sports moment? How did you feel when it happened?

- ▶▶▶ Write about a time your team won an important game. Now write about a time you lost a game. Share the differences in how you felt during each experience.

AUTHOR BIOGRAPHY

Brandon Terrell is the author of numerous books and graphic novels, ranging from sports stories to spooky tales to mind-boggling mysteries. When not hunched over his laptop writing, Brandon enjoys watching movies and television, reading, cooking, and spending time with his wife and two children in Minnesota.

ILLUSTRATOR BIOGRAPHY

Fran Bueno was born and lives in Santiago de Compostela in Spain. Since he was a little kid, he has loved comic books. He was reading *El Jabato* at age eight, a comic book that his father always bought him, and in that exact moment he decided to become an artist. He studied at art school and will always be grateful to his parents for supporting him. His motivation is to do what he does best and enjoys most. He loves traveling with his wife and kids, being with friends, books, music, movies, and TV shows. Just a regular guy? He would agree.

CHECK OUT ALL 4 BOOKS IN THIS SERIES!

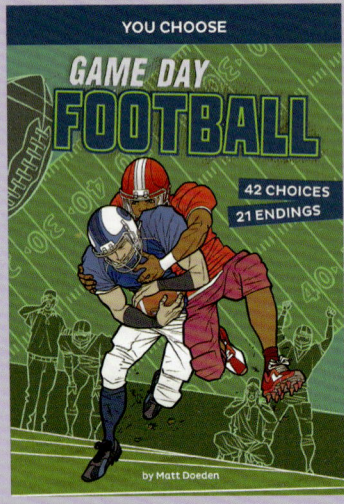
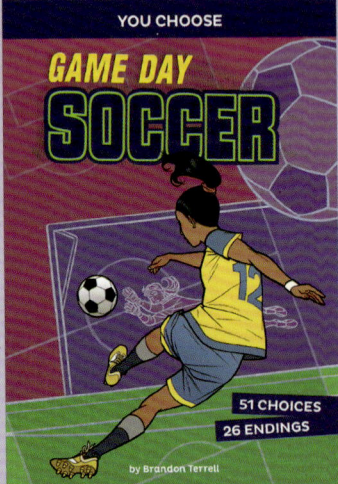

YOU CHOOSE

GAME DAY
FOOTBALL

AN INTERACTIVE SPORTS STORY

BY MATT DOEDEN
ILLUSTRATED BY FRAN BUENO

CAPSTONE PRESS
a capstone imprint

You Choose Books are published by Capstone Press, an imprint of Capstone.
1710 Roe Crest Drive
North Mankato, Minnesota 56003
www.capstonepub.com

Copyright © 2021 by Capstone Press, a Capstone imprint. All rights reserved. No part of this publication may be reproduced in whole or in part, or stored in a retrieval system, or transmitted in any form or by any means, electronic, mechanical, photocopying, recording, or otherwise, without written permission of the publisher.

Library of Congress Cataloging-in-Publication Data
Names: Doeden, Matt, author. | Bueno, Fran, illustrator.
Title: Game day football : an interactive sports story / by Matt Doeden ; [illustrated by Fran Bueno].
Description: North Mankato, Minnesota : Capstone Press, [2021] | Series: You choose: Game day sports | Audience: Ages 8-11. | Audience: Grades 4-6. | Summary: Facing down a mighty opponent on the football field, the reader's choices can mean the difference between a triumphant victory and a heartbreaking loss.
Identifiers: LCCN 2020039300 (print) | LCCN 2020039301 (ebook) | ISBN 9781496696038 (hardcover) | ISBN 9781496697127 (paperback) | ISBN 9781977154279 (ebook pdf)
Subjects: LCSH: Plot-your-own stories. | CYAC: Football--Fiction. | Plot-your-own stories.
Classification: LCC PZ8.D6663 Gam 2021 (print) | LCC PZ8.D6663 (ebook) | DDC [Fic]--dc23
LC record available at https://lccn.loc.gov/2020039300
LC ebook record available at https://lccn.loc.gov/2020039301

Editorial Credits
Editor: Angie Kaelberer; Designer: Kayla Rossow; Media Researcher: Eric Gohl; Premedia Specialist: Katy LaVigne

Printed and bound in China. PO6238

TABLE OF CONTENTS

About Your Game 5

CHAPTER 1
Game Time 7

CHAPTER 2
High School Hero 11

CHAPTER 3
College Championship................ 41

CHAPTER 4
Super Bowl Superstar................ 67

CHAPTER 5
An All-American Game 101

Glossary 106
Test Your Football Knowledge 107
Discussion Questions 110
Author Biography 111
Illustrator Biography 111

ABOUT YOUR GAME

YOU are about to step onto the field for the biggest football game of your life. You're playing for the championship, and every decision you make will affect the outcome. Will you be aggressive? Or will you play it safe? Can you protect a lead? Or will you need to lead a big comeback? YOU CHOOSE what happens on the field. Do you have what it takes?

Chapter 1 sets the scene. Then you choose which path to read. Follow the directions at the bottom of the page as you read the stories. The decisions you make will change your outcome. After you finish one path, go back and read the others for new perspectives and more adventures.

CHAPTER 1
GAME TIME

The locker room smells of sweat. A heavy hip-hop beat thumps as you and your teammates prepare to take the field for the biggest game of your lives.

As you strap on your shoulder pads, you close your eyes. You picture yourself standing on the field. The crowd is roaring as the ball is snapped. The game is on the line, and it's up to you to make the play. You imagine every detail. You picture yourself making the play. Winning the game. Celebrating with your teammates. You take a slow, deep breath.

Turn the page.

You stand up and pull your jersey over your head. "Are we ready?" you shout.

Together, your teammates respond, "We are ready!" Then everyone begins to shout and howl. You slap each other's helmets. You slam your pads into each other. You work yourselves into a frenzy.

Your head coach looks on with a smile. This is your team's pregame ritual. It's how you prepare yourselves. It's how you get charged up.

"Then let's go!" you shout.

As a unit, the team charges out of the locker room, following your lead. Together, you burst out onto the field, soaking in the roar of the crowd.

It's game time, and a championship is on the line. Do you have what it takes to claim it?

To play linebacker for your high school in the conference title game, turn to page 11.

To be a running back in the National Collegiate Athletic Association (NCAA) championship, turn to page 41.

To lead your team in the Super Bowl as a quarterback, turn to page 67.

CHAPTER 2
HIGH SCHOOL HERO

Your heart is pumping as you peer into your opponent's backfield from your position at middle linebacker. In the background, you hear the roar of the crowd and the beat of your team's fight song. The smell of damp grass and mud drifts up from the trampled field. You glance to your left, where your best friend, Teddy, prepares to rush the quarterback from his spot at defensive end.

It's the second quarter of the conference championship. You're facing East High, the best team in the state. Nobody thinks your team has a chance of winning.

Turn the page.

East's players are bigger, faster, and more experienced. They've won five straight conference titles, and they haven't lost a game all season.

Yet through more than a quarter, your team has kept up with the champs. The game's tied 3–3. Their all-state quarterback barks out signals as a wide receiver motions to the left. Your body is tense, ready to drop back into pass coverage. Your coach is expecting a passing play, and your job is to cover the middle of the field.

As you look at East's formation, something clicks in your mind. You've seen this formation before. They used it early in the first quarter on a running play. On that play, the running back gashed through your defense for a big gain. Are they going back to the same play?

What should you do? Do you stick with the play call and drop into pass coverage? Or do you charge the line of scrimmage, ready to tackle the running back? The quarterback shouts out his signals, and the center snaps the ball. You have to decide now.

To stick with the play call and fall into coverage, turn to page 14.

To charge forward to stop the run, turn to page 16.

A defense only works if every defender is on the same page. There's no time to change the play call. You have to do your job.

East's quarterback takes the snap. You watch him as you backpedal, gaining depth. The running back comes up to take a handoff, but the quarterback pulls the ball back. It's a play action—a fake run designed to trick the defense into crowding the line.

The opposing tight end is streaking across the field. You charge toward him, just as the quarterback throws the ball.

You dive, stretching out your arm and knocking down the ball. Incomplete pass!

You did your job. East's drive is over, and your offense is going to get a turn. They march down the field for a touchdown. Your big play helps your team go into halftime with a 10–3 lead.

But the game is far from over. East opens the second half with the ball. They're moving down the field. Your coach calls a blitz. Your job is to rush the quarterback.

You get a good jump once the ball is snapped. You charge through the line. You're just a few steps away as the quarterback begins to throw the ball. You'll never make it in time.

To pull up and track the ball in the air, turn to page 19.
To hit the quarterback as hard as you can, turn to page 26.

"I know this play," you whisper to yourself. You've seen the formation. You're sure it's going to be a run. So when the ball is snapped, you spring into action. Instead of dropping back to defend the pass, you charge into a gap on the left side of the line.

As you run, you look into the backfield. The running back reaches out to take the handoff from the quarterback. You've got him!

But then the quarterback pulls the ball back. It's a play action—a fake run! The quarterback zips the ball over the middle to a wide-open receiver. There's nobody to stop him. All you can do is watch as the receiver dances into the end zone.

Turn the page.

"What are you doing?" Teddy asks as you walk off the field. "Get your head in the game!"

The big play gets East rolling. By halftime, your team is down, 17–6. The second half starts out much the same way. East is driving down the field. On a big third-down play, the quarterback sets up to throw over the middle. It's coming your way.

To cut in front of the receiver to go for an interception, turn to page 21.

To set up for a big hit on the receiver, turn to page 24.

As badly as you want to hit the quarterback, you can't do it now. It would be a sure penalty, and you'd be risking injury to both of you. So you pull up and spin around, just in time to watch the receiver drop the pass. It's incomplete! East is forced to kick a field goal, and your team still leads, 10–6.

That's where the score stays for the rest of the quarter. The third quarter is a defensive battle. No one scores any points. But the action picks up in the fourth quarter. Your offense kicks a field goal, and East answers with a touchdown. It's tied 13–13 as the clock continues to run. Time is running short.

"Let's go!" Teddy shouts as the defense takes the field after a stalled drive. "Come on, let's get our offense one more shot."

Turn the page.

You do all you can, but East always feels a step ahead. They move the ball with ease. The clock reads 2:00, and East has a first down at your 12-yard line.

East snaps the ball. It's a running play. The running back darts through the line, picking up five quick yards. As he streaks toward the sideline, you manage to wrap your left arm around his waist.

> To try to strip the ball from the running back, turn to page 23.
>
> To make a sure tackle, turn to page 28.

You make the split-second decision to go for the interception. You charge into the passing lane. Just as you expected, the quarterback releases the ball. You're ready. You reach out and snag the ball out of the air at a full run. You don't slow down, weaving your way through the opposing players and streaking into the end zone. Touchdown! Just like that, it's 17–13. Your team is back in the game.

It gets even better in the fourth quarter when your team returns a punt for a touchdown. With four minutes to play, you're ahead, 20–17. East charges back, driving deep into your territory. With just fourteen seconds left on the clock, East faces fourth down from the 2-yard line. They could kick a field goal to tie it. But they go for the win instead. It all comes down to this play.

Turn the page.

East's quarterback takes the snap and rolls to his right. You close the distance as he scans for an open receiver. Behind you, the tight end is streaking across the field into the end zone. In front of you, the quarterback looks like he might tuck the ball and run for the score.

Everything rides on your decision.

To go for the quarterback, turn to page 38.
To fall back to cover the tight end in the end zone, turn to page 39.

Your team is running out of time. A tackle here will stop the play, but the drive will keep going. You have to do something big. So instead of wrapping up the runner for a tackle, you swing your right arm down. Your open palm slams straight down on the ball, jarring it loose.

Fumble! The ball bounces back up in the air, straight into your arms. You stand there in shock for half a second. Then you hear Teddy screaming from behind you. "Run! Run!"

You charge down the field. A wall of East players is coming at you. You're not going to get far. Out of the corner of your eye, you see one of your cornerbacks coming up fast toward the left sideline. You don't see anyone in front of him.

> To pitch the ball to your teammate, turn to page 30.
> To keep running for yards, turn to page 32.

You lower your shoulder. At the moment the ball arrives, you slam your body into the receiver. The massive hit jars the ball loose—incomplete pass.

You lie on the ground. You're dizzy. Everything seems to be moving in slow motion.

"Awesome hit!" Teddy says, grabbing your hand and helping you to your feet. The world is spinning. "Shake it off," Teddy says. "Come on, we've got this!"

You pause for a second to catch your breath. Your head hurts. You can't seem to focus your vision.

> To take yourself out of the game, turn to page 34.
> To shake it off and keep playing, turn to page 36.

Your frustration boils over. You've watched this quarterback complete too many passes. It's time to put him on the ground. You launch yourself at him, even though he's already released the ball. The top of your helmet slams into the side of his.

You both go down in a heap. Yellow flags fly through the air.

"Personal foul, number 55 on the defense," announces the referee, calling out your jersey number. "Fifteen yards. This is a targeting foul. Number 55 is ejected from the game."

"Come on!" Teddy hisses at you with disgust. "What were you thinking?"

Your teammates look at you with disappointment as you walk off the field, your head hanging low. You go back to the locker room and sit on the bench with your head in your hands. Without you on the field, your team can't stop East's powerful offense. By the time it's over, East is celebrating yet another championship. Your teammates barely look at you. Your coach just shakes his head.

It was the biggest opportunity of your football career, and you blew it.

THE END

To follow another path, turn to page 9.
To learn more about football, turn to page 101.

The running back tries to break free, but you wrap both arms around his waist and drive him to the ground. The whistle blows to signal the end of the play, but the clock keeps ticking.

"Nice tackle," says your opponent, giving you a gentle slap on the shoulder pad.

You look up. The clock keeps ticking, and your team is out of time-outs. You can't stop it. East runs it again on each of the next two plays. You stop both runs for short gains. But the clock doesn't stop moving. It ticks down toward zero as the field-goal unit comes onto the field. It's a short kick, and East's all-state kicker boots it through.

You can only watch in silence as the East players storm the field to celebrate yet another conference championship. Teddy puts his arm around you. "So close," he says. "I thought we had it."

You shake your head. It's going to take a long time to get over the sting of this loss.

THE END
To follow another path, turn to page 9.
To learn more about football, turn to page 101.

Before anyone can tackle you, you pivot your body and pitch the ball back and to the left. You're certain that your teammate will be able to score.

But then it all goes terribly wrong. The pitch never even makes it to your teammate. One of East's receivers steps right into the path of the ball, snatching it out of the air. The crowd roars as the receiver streaks into the end zone. Touchdown!

"Oh no," you grunt as you realize what you've done. On the sideline, all you see is your coach bent over at the waist, with his hands on his head.

It was one of the wildest, most exciting plays of the year. It's a play that everyone will be talking about for years to come. And, unfortunately, it's a play that costs your team a shot at the championship.

THE END

To follow another path, turn to page 9.
To learn more about football, turn to page 101.

You tuck the ball tightly against your body and charge into the wave of tacklers. One man hits you. You keep charging. Another. And another. You don't stop moving your legs, picking up every yard you can, driving your way almost to midfield. Finally, they bring you down. You're crushed at the bottom of a pile of bodies, but you feel great after making the play.

Your offense rushes onto the field. They're charged up after your big fumble recovery. They strike quickly, moving the ball in big chunks against the stunned East defense. Your field-goal kicker boots the game winner as the clock strikes zero, and you rush onto the field. Teddy wraps you up in a giant bear hug. "You did it!" he roars.

You give him a celebratory slap on the back. "We did it!"

The celebration is just getting started. Your team is the conference champion, and you're the game's MVP. It's a moment you'll never forget.

THE END
To follow another path, turn to page 9.
To learn more about football, turn to page 101.

You stumble. The world is spinning. You go down to one knee and wave at the team's trainer, Erika.

"Are you all right?" she asks. You shake your head.

Erika and Teddy help you to your feet. Erika asks you some questions and shines a light in your eyes. "It looks like a concussion," she says. "We need to get you to a doctor."

Your team rallies around you. "Go win this thing!" you tell them as you leave the field with Erika's help.

"Don't worry, we'll do it for you," Teddy promises.

And that's what your team does. As you're headed to the hospital for tests, Teddy leads an amazing comeback. And they dedicate it all to you. More good news comes from your tests. The concussion isn't too severe, and there's no bleeding. "I want you to take it easy for a few days," says the doctor as she looks at your chart. "But I don't see any reason that you won't recover fully."

It was a close call, but you'll be OK. And as you leave the hospital, your entire team is lined up to greet you. Teddy gives you the game ball. You can't stop smiling.

THE END
To follow another path, turn to page 9.
To learn more about football, turn to page 101.

You shake your head and slap yourself in the helmet. You're too tough to come out of the game now. It's too important.

The next play is a run. You feel a little slow, but the play comes right to you. You go low and dive in for the tackle.

Then everything goes black. You're unconscious as the trainers rush onto the field. You don't remember the stretcher, the ambulance, or the ride to the hospital.

What you do remember is seeing your coach when you wake up in a hospital bed. He leans over and takes your hand. "You've had a severe concussion," he explains. "A very serious bruise to your brain. I'm sorry, but I'm afraid your playing days are over. Right now, we just want you to get better."

Football was a battle. Now you're starting a battle of a different kind.

THE END
To follow another path, turn to page 9.
To learn more about football, turn to page 101.

37

You can't be in two places. You have to make the quarterback throw it. You put your head down and charge.

He stops running. He backpedals. You're closing in. Three steps away . . . two steps. He tries to spin away, but you're ready. You open your arms and launch yourself into his midsection. The crunch of pads crashing into pads is the sweetest sound you've ever heard. You drive him backward, into the turf.

The whistle blows. It's a sack! The drive is over. You've won! Your team swarms out onto the field, celebrating the biggest win in the school's history. The crowd roars. The coach wraps you up in a bear hug, and then Teddy lifts you up onto his shoulders.

It's the play of a lifetime, and a game you'll never forget.

THE END

To follow another path, turn to page 9.
To learn more about football, turn to page 101.

You're caught in a tough situation. If you chase the quarterback, you leave the tight end wide open. So you pivot and change direction to cover the tight end.

You watch over your shoulder as you run. East's quarterback watches you drop back. He knows exactly what to do. He runs for it.

It's too late for you to do anything about it. Nobody can stop him. He prances into the end zone as the East fans go wild.

You came so close. You almost had it. But in the end, you came up just a little short. Good wasn't good enough. You needed to be great.

THE END

To follow another path, turn to page 9.
To learn more about football, turn to page 101.

CHAPTER 3
COLLEGE CHAMPIONSHIP

"Have you ever seen anything like this?" asks your teammate Antonio. The two of you are standing on the field waiting for the College Football Playoff National Championship to begin. It's the biggest event in NCAA football. The stands are packed. TV cameras are everywhere. A famous pop singer sang the national anthem. A formation of U.S. fighter planes just streaked overhead.

You shake your head. You've been in big games before. You've played in packed stadiums. But this is another level. The stands are packed with fans, and all of them seem to be screaming.

Turn the page.

"Well, just another game," Antonio says, smacking your helmet. "Let's go get it!"

Your team won the coin toss and received the opening kickoff. Now it's time to see what your offense can do against the Alabama Crimson Tide defense—the biggest, fastest defense in the nation.

Antonio calls the first play—a run. You smile. You're the team's starting running back, and you can't wait to see if you can cut and weave through this defense loaded with future NFL talent.

The sound of the crowd is deafening as Antonio calls out the signals. The defenders crowd the line of scrimmage, ready to rush.

The center snaps the ball. Antonio flips it to you as you run to the right. A defender closes in on you, but you manage to juke out of his way.

As you run by him, you see a lot of open field in front of you. You turn on the jets, streaking down the field, picking up ten . . . twenty . . . thirty yards.

The Alabama safety is coming at you fast. He's setting up for a massive hit.

To step out-of-bounds, turn to page 44.

To put your head down and absorb the big hit, turn to page 46.

It's a big gain, but you're not going any farther. You quickly step out-of-bounds, half a second before the Alabama safety can reach you.

It's a great start, and your team finishes the drive with a field goal to take the lead. It marks the beginning of a defensive battle. Alabama ties in the second quarter and then takes a 6–3 lead in the third.

Late in the fourth quarter, your team has the ball near midfield. That's when your coach calls the play you've been practicing for weeks. It's a trick play, and if you can pull it off, it could make all the difference.

Antonio takes the snap and pitches you the ball as you run to the right. The defense is crashing in, blowing past your line's blocks. But that's by design, because you're not really running the ball. You're passing it.

The Alabama defense reacts quickly. Your primary receiver, the tight end, is slanting across the middle of the field. A linebacker is just a step behind him. It's a tight passing window, and you're not sure you can pull it off. But as the defense collapses, you don't have time to wait.

To make the risky throw, turn to page 52.
To tuck the ball away and prepare to be tackled, turn to page 64.

You want to get every last yard. So you lower your head and shoulders and prepare for impact.

The safety slams into you with incredible speed. The hit sends you down hard and knocks the ball from your grasp. Desperately, you try to reach out to pull in the ball. But it's already out of reach.

You hit the ground with a thump. An Alabama player scoops up the fumble and runs it back for a touchdown. As the defense is celebrating, you're gasping for breath. The hit knocked the wind out of you. For a moment, you feel like you're suffocating. But it passes. You're able to get up and walk off the field.

As the team's trainers check you out, the offense takes the field without you. Tyler, the backup running back, electrifies the crowd by catching a screen pass and running it in for a touchdown to tie the game. You're happy, but you hate that you're watching from the sidelines.

To tell your coach that you're ready to play, turn to page 48.

To take the rest of the half off and come back in the third quarter, turn to page 55.

"I'm good to go, Coach," you say. "Just got the wind knocked out of me."

The game turns into an offensive shoot-out. You lead a grinding running attack that wears down the Alabama defense. But every time you score, Alabama comes back to answer with a score of their own.

With just three minutes remaining in the fourth quarter, the game is tied, 31–31. Your team has driven the ball all the way down to the Alabama 2-yard line. It's fourth down, and your coach has decided to go for it.

"Let's punch this thing in!" Antonio shouts in the huddle. He calls for an off-tackle running play. That means you'll be carrying the ball straight into the heart of the defense. It will be power versus power in the biggest play of the game.

Turn the page.

The stadium is deafening as Antonio calls out the signals. A wide receiver motions to the left. Antonio takes the snap. You charge forward, taking the handoff and driving into the pile of bodies in front of you. For a moment, you spot a seam in the defense. But it closes just as soon as you get to it. You're at the 1-yard line, and you know you won't be able to power your way into the end zone. You've got to do something, or the drive ends here.

To try to cut back and search for another running lane, go to page 51.

To extend your arm to reach the ball over the goal line, turn to page 57.

The running lane is closed. There are too many bodies in your way. You'll never make it through. So you bounce back and dart to your left, searching for another way into the end zone.

The defense swarms. Your blockers are all locked up in the middle of the field. There's no one out here to protect you. You stop, backpedal, and try reversing your field by running to the right. More defenders await there. You're trapped. One defender gets an arm around your waist. Another wraps up your legs.

You keep fighting, but you have no chance. A third defender slams into you, sending you backward to the turf in a hard, painful tackle. You groan as the defender does a celebratory dance. The drive is over. And you're running out of time.

Turn to page 53.

Your offense is struggling. You've had trouble moving the ball the whole game, and you need to take a chance. You loft a high rainbow pass over the pass rushers. The ball sails through the air and comes down, right in your tight end's outstretched arms. He bulls ahead for a big 25-yard gain to put your team in field-goal range.

"Yeah!" Antonio screams as you run down the field to set up your next play.

"See, passing isn't so hard," you tell him with a smirk. "Anyone can do it."

Your big pass proves to be important, because the drive stalls there. The kicking unit comes onto the field to attempt the critical field goal.

The snap and hold are perfect, and the kicker boots it long and straight, right through the uprights. The game is tied, 6–6.

Alabama takes over possession as the final minutes of the fourth quarter tick away. Your defense is tired, and the Crimson Tide march down the field with a series of short passing plays. With fifteen seconds left, they kick a field goal to surge ahead by three points.

You have one last shot. Antonio calls a passing play. As you step to the line, the crowd is beyond loud. You can feel your blood pumping, knowing this is the last shot you're going to get.

You get set in your stance as Antonio screams out his signals. You can barely hear him over the roar of the crowd.

Turn the page.

Antonio takes the snap and drops back. Everything feels like it's happening in slow motion. You scan the field, watching the receivers streak down the field. Your linemen are doing all they can to block, but Alabama's pass rush is coming hard. There isn't going to be much time. Everything has come down to this play.

> To run a short route over the middle of the field, turn to page 60.
>
> To stay and block for Antonio, turn to page 62.

You still don't feel like you're completely recovered from the big hit. And Tyler is capable of carrying the ball for the rest of this half.

In fact, he's more than capable. He's on fire. He scores again on the next drive. Then he adds a third touchdown just before halftime. It's 21–7, and your backup is doing it all!

"I'm ready, put me back in there," you tell your coach at halftime.

He smiles at you and puts a hand on your shoulder. "I don't think so," he says. "I think you still need to recover."

"No, I swear, I'm good to go," you say.

He looks you in the eye. "Sorry. I have to go with the hot hand. The official word will be that you're still dinged up."

Turn the page.

And so you watch the second half from the sideline. Tyler is the game's MVP. He's the breakout star, and his performance is all anyone can talk about.

The good news is that you're a member of the NCAA championship team. You just wish you'd experienced more than one play of the big game.

THE END
To follow another path, turn to page 9.
To learn more about football, turn to page 101.

You won't be able to run over the goal line, but you just might be able to reach it. Bodies crash into you from every side, but you surge forward with both arms, reaching the ball out as far as you can.

Everything happens in a flash. A defender slams into you just as you're reaching. You can feel the ball come free of your grasp. After a moment of confusion, the whistle blows. The referee signals TOUCHDOWN!

It was a risky play, but you managed to get the ball over the goal line before the defender could knock it out. After the extra point, your team leads, 38–31. Alabama desperately tries to come back on its final drive, but your defense steps up. You get the ball back with just twenty seconds left on the clock.

Turn the page.

Antonio takes the snap and drops to a knee. Alabama can't stop the clock, so the game is over. Your team storms the field as the fans go wild. You're the national champions! You came up big in the most important game of your life.

THE END

To follow another path, turn to page 9.
To learn more about football, turn to page 101.

Antonio might need a checkdown receiver in case none of the deep receivers get open. So you run a simple slant route over the middle of the field. You put your arms up as defenders break through the line.

Antonio has nowhere to go. Half a second before two pass rushers bury him in a bone-crunching tackle, he flings the ball to you. You snatch it out of the air and turn to run. You pick up ten . . . twenty . . . thirty yards. But then you hit a wave of defenders.

You realize your mistake. You can't make it to the end zone, and time is running out. You try to weave through the wall of defenders, but you have no chance. They all tackle you, bringing you to the ground as time runs out.

The players on Alabama's sideline rush onto the field to celebrate their national title. All you can do is lay on the ground, clutching the ball, wondering how the game got away from you.

THE END

To follow another path, turn to page 9.
To learn more about football, turn to page 101.

A short pass won't do you any good. You've got to help protect Antonio.

As Antonio scans the field, an Alabama defensive end slips past his blocker. He's got a free run at the quarterback. But you're there. You throw your body into his path. He's much bigger than you, and you only slow him down a little bit. But it's enough. Your block gives Antonio another half of a second.

He spots a receiver and flings the ball deep. It sails through the air, right into the arms of the receiver. Touchdown! You raise your arms in the air and look up at the clock. It reads 0:00. The game is over!

Antonio is screaming as he lifts you off of the ground. "We did it! We did it!"

"What a throw!" you shout back.

"What a block!" he replies.

It's the play of the year. And none of it could have happened if you hadn't done your job and protected your quarterback.

THE END
To follow another path, turn to page 9.
To learn more about football, turn to page 101.

The passing lane is too tight. A quarterback might be able to make that throw, but you're no quarterback. So instead of risking an interception, you secure the ball and dive forward, just as two defenders slam into you.

The play was a failure. The drive stalls, and Alabama takes possession. You watch helplessly from the sideline as the Crimson Tide ram the ball down the throat of your defense with one run after another. The clock ticks away. With less than a minute to go, Alabama seals the game with a touchdown.

It's all over. You tried your best. But today, that wasn't good enough. Second place will have to be enough this year.

THE END

To follow another path, turn to page 9.
To learn more about football, turn to page 101.

CHAPTER 4
SUPER BOWL SUPERSTAR

You were never supposed to be here. You're about to face the Los Angeles Rams in the Super Bowl—one of the biggest sporting events in the world. And you're an undrafted rookie who was never expected to make the team.

But after a good preseason, you did make the team as the third-string quarterback. When the starter broke his leg in the first game of the season, you became the backup. And when Marshall, the new starter, separated his shoulder in the final game of the regular season, you became the starter.

Turn the page.

Even then, you weren't supposed to be here. Your team squeaked into the playoffs at 9–7. Your first start came in a playoff game. And you've been doing nothing but scoring touchdowns ever since. Somehow, you've led your team to the biggest game in the world. And now you have a chance to do the unthinkable.

"Be smart," says your coach. He's a former NFL quarterback himself, and he's been a key to your success. "No turnovers. You don't have to win this game for us. Just don't lose it."

Marshall gives you a nod. His shoulder is healed now, but the coach has stuck with you as the starter.

After winning the coin toss, you take the field for your first drive. Camera flashes light up the stands. The roar of the crowd shakes the ground.

The first play is a run-pass option. As you line up, you look out at the Los Angeles defense. You pay special attention to the linebackers. Will they drop into coverage or crowd the line? What will you do if they blitz?

You call out your signals and take the snap. You roll to the right, staying behind your blockers as they fight to fend off the pass rushers. On the opposite side of the field, your tight end breaks free of the defensive coverage. If you can get a throw through the heavy traffic in front of you, it could be a big play. But throwing across the field is risky. It might be better to run.

To run the ball, turn to page 70.
To throw it, turn to page 72.

It's too risky of a throw. So instead you use your feet, spinning your way past three defenders before finally being tackled. It's a seven-yard gain—not bad for the first play of the game.

It's a blueprint you follow throughout the first half. The Los Angeles defense is set to defend the pass, so you use a heavy dose of running to chew up yardage. Meanwhile, your defense does its best to contain their strong offense. You go into halftime tied, 10–10.

Late in the third quarter, you face a third-and-five. The defense has been rushing hard. So you use their aggressive play against them by using a hard count. You use your voice to trick the defensive line into thinking you're snapping the ball. One of them bites, jumping offsides.

Your center instantly snaps you the ball as yellow flags fly. It's a free play. You can always take the penalty. But it's also a chance to get more. One of your receivers is double-covered twenty yards down the field. A second is open on a short crossing route. Where should you throw it?

To throw deep, turn to page 75.
To take the safe, short throw, turn to page 76.

You can't resist the chance for a big play. You pivot your body and fling a pass. But you're throwing in the opposite direction than you're running. The pass is on target. But it doesn't have much zip on it.

Before the ball ever reaches your receiver, a Rams linebacker steps into the passing lane. He snags it out of the air and starts running. It all happens so fast that no one can stop him. It's an interception for a touchdown on the first play of the game! This couldn't have started any worse.

The only good news is that your team immediately gets the ball back. You won't have to wait long to redeem yourself. Your offense works the ball down the field with a series of runs and short passes. You face third down and eight yards to go from midfield.

Turn the page.

Coach calls for a passing play. But none of your receivers is open, so you take off running.

You quickly pick up five yards. A defender is bearing down on you. He's eager to hit you. Hard. You can slide to protect yourself, but you won't get the first down. Or you can take your chances with a big hit.

> To try for the first down, turn to page 77.
> To slide, turn to page 83.

It's a free play. That means it's time to go for the touchdown. You step into the throw, firing the ball as hard as you can down the sideline. Your receiver leaps into the air and makes an amazing one-handed catch. His defender stumbles, leaving no one to stop him. You scream as he cruises into the end zone. Touchdown! Just like that, your team is ahead, 17–10!

In the fourth quarter, you focus on the run. The goal is to chew up the clock and protect your lead. And it's working. Soon, just two minutes remain in the game. You've got the ball, but it's third down and seven.

Los Angeles is out of time-outs. So a running play will use up a lot more time. But you've got a much better chance to get the first down—and end the game—with a pass.

To run and use up game time, turn to page 93.
To try to get the first down with a pass, turn to page 95.

You decide to play it safe, throwing to the open receiver. It's a six-yard gain—just one more yard than the penalty would have earned you. On the sideline, your coach has his head in his hands. You know he thinks that you missed a big opportunity.

And he's probably right. The Los Angeles pass rush sacks you on the next play, and the drive stalls. You're forced to punt. A few minutes later, the Rams score a touchdown to take a seven-point lead. The third quarter expires. You have just fifteen minutes left to get back in the game.

Turn to page 81.

Quarterbacks often slide to protect themselves from big hits. But this is the Super Bowl, and you're already behind. So instead of sliding, you launch yourself into the air. The defender slams into you with a huge hit, but he can't stop your forward progress.

You wince a little as you stand up. Your whole body hurts. But the referee signals first down. The drive is still alive. Three plays later, you cash in with a touchdown pass to your running back. "That's the way!" Coach says, giving you a smack on the helmet as you come off the field.

Late in the third quarter, the game is tied, 17–17. Your defense just got an interception. You're already at the Los Angeles 40-yard line. Coach calls for a long passing play.

Turn the page.

The center snaps you the ball, and you drop back seven steps. You have a receiver streaking down each sideline. The receiver on the left side has half a step on his defender. You reach back and hurl the ball down the field. It zips through the air. But your throw is just a tiny bit short. The defensive back leaps and grabs the ball with both hands. He's off to the races, zigging and zagging along the sideline.

The Los Angeles players are all setting up blocks. They're bigger and stronger, and getting in their way is dangerous.

To stay clear of the blockers, turn to page 80.
To try to make the tackle, turn to page 84.

You're not going to be able to make the tackle. Los Angeles has a wall of blockers in front of the defensive back, and nobody can stop him. You watch helplessly as the Rams return the interception for a touchdown. Los Angeles takes a seven-point lead into the fourth quarter.

"Don't worry about it," says Coach as you return to the sidelines. "You'll get another shot at it."

Go to page 81.

Both defenses lock down in the final quarter. You trade punt after punt as the clock ticks away. With two minutes to play, you get the ball. You need a touchdown.

That's when your running back delivers. He bursts through the line and gashes the defense. He speeds all the way to the Los Angeles 5-yard line. The clock ticks under a minute.

Two plays later, you face third down from the 1-yard line. Only fifteen seconds remain. You take the snap and run a quarterback sneak. You stay low and punch the ball into the end zone. It's a one-point game!

> To go for a two-point conversion, turn to page 82.
> To kick the extra point and force overtime, turn to page 87.

Your coach loves to gamble. Most coaches would kick the extra point. But he signals for you to go for the two-point conversion. That means that it all comes down to one play. Make it, and you win. Fail, and you lose.

The crowd is on its feet. You can't even hear yourself call the signals at the line of scrimmage. The defense is shifting and pointing out assignments.

The plan is to throw to your tight end in the corner of the end zone. But as you take the snap, two linebackers blitz. Your running back blocks one of them, but the other is coming free.

Your tight end is still running his route. You need another second, but the blitzing linebacker is about to hit you.

To try to run for the end zone, turn to page 89.
To throw the pass, turn to page 92.
To scramble to buy more time for a pass, turn to page 98.

You're about to get destroyed. So you do a baseball-style slide, ending the play and preventing the defenders from hitting you.

You needed eight yards. You got only six. The punt team comes on. You watch as the Rams take possession and march down the field for another touchdown. Just like that, you're behind, 14–0. And it only gets worse from there. By halftime, you're getting blown out, 27–3.

"Sorry," says Coach. "I'm putting Marshall into the game. We need something to change."

Marshall leads the team to a spirited second-half comeback. But the Rams hold on for a 30–24 victory.

You came up short. You're not sure you'll ever get another chance.

THE END
To follow another path, turn to page 9.
To learn more about football, turn to page 101.

Your football instincts kick in. You have to make the tackle. You charge toward the sideline. But your effort is hopeless. A linebacker lowers his shoulder and blasts you with a bone-crunching block. It sends you flying like a rag doll. Your helmet slams hard onto the turf.

Everything goes hazy. Your vision blurs. You feel dizzy and sick to your stomach. You lie on the turf for several minutes as trainers check you out.

"You've got a concussion," they tell you. "We need to get you to the hospital."

"No . . . I can play," you insist.

Coach shakes his head. "Sorry. League rules. We've got to keep you safe."

Turn the page.

Without you in the game, the offense falls apart. Los Angeles runs up the score and earns an easy victory.

The doctors tell you that you'll recover. But you know that your best chance to win the Super Bowl just slipped away. You can only hope that someday you'll get another one.

THE END
To follow another path, turn to page 9.
To learn more about football, turn to page 101.

After a quick celebration with your offensive line, you trot back to the sideline. You watch as your kicker boots the extra point to tie the game. It's on to overtime!

Los Angeles wins the coin toss and takes the kickoff. The kick returner speeds up the middle of the field and then cuts left. He spins away from a tackler. Then he outruns another. He streaks down the sideline as the crowd goes wild.

Your heart sinks. Nobody can catch him. The Los Angeles players surge onto the field to celebrate one of the most thrilling plays in Super Bowl history.

Turn the page.

You did all that work to force overtime. And you never even got to touch the ball! You stand there on the sideline, staring in stunned silence. It's the most painful loss you've ever had. But you vow that you'll be back next year, and you're going to win it all.

THE END

To follow another path, turn to page 9.
To learn more about football, turn to page 101.

You're out of time. Just before the linebacker slams into you, you tuck the ball away and dart to the left. Defenders come crashing in from all sides as you search for a running lane.

You don't have many choices. All you can do is cut up the field. You quickly fake a pass, even though you have no open receivers. The fake is just enough to slow down the defense, though. You sprint forward. You're five yards away . . . four . . . three.

Defenders are coming from each side. You launch yourself into the air. A defender hits you, spinning you around as you fly through the air. But the hit isn't enough to stop your momentum. You sail over the goal line . . . just barely. You made it!

Turn the page.

The roar of the crowd is deafening. Your teammates are rushing over to pile on top of you.

You did it! It's one of the most thrilling plays in Super Bowl history, and a game that no one will ever forget. In just one season, you've gone from undrafted rookie to Super Bowl MVP. And your career is just beginning. You can't wait to see what comes next.

THE END

To follow another path, turn to page 9.
To learn more about football, turn to page 101.

You can't wait. You have to throw it now. You loft the ball, putting a little extra arc on it to give your tight end time to get under it.

But it's hopeless. The defensive back has too much time to adjust. He times his leap perfectly, batting the ball to the ground. Incomplete pass.

Game over.

It feels like a punch to the gut. You fall to your knees on the turf, watching the Rams celebrate. You were so close. Just another half second was all you needed. This loss is going to hurt for a long time.

THE END
To follow another path, turn to page 9.
To learn more about football, turn to page 101.

Right now, using up the time on the clock is more important than gaining yards. The crowd is roaring as you step to the line. The defense is going to come hard. But you're ready. You take the snap and roll right. You hang behind your blockers as long as you can, not caring that you'll lose a few yards. Finally, the defense breaks through. You dive to the ground, securing the ball.

The clock keeps running. It's down to 1:20 by the time your punt team comes on. Your punter gives a beautiful kick, pinning the Rams inside their own 20-yard line.

Turn the page.

You watch from the sideline as Los Angeles desperately tries to come back. But with no time-outs left, they run out of time. As the final seconds tick away, you and your teammates dump a bucket of ice water on your coach's head. "We did it!" you shout, hugging him.

It was the biggest game of your life, and you gave it all you had. You're a Super Bowl champion. And best of all, you have a bright career in front of you.

THE END

To follow another path, turn to page 9.
To learn more about football, turn to page 101.

A first down here would end it. You step to the line and see that the defense is expecting a run. You smile. You're confident that you have them now.

You shout out your signals over the roar of the crowd. You take the snap and drop back three steps. Your receiver is running a quick slant. The pass rush is blasting through your offensive line, and there's no time to waste. You sling a pass over the middle, right into the hands of your receiver.

But he drops it. "No!" you shout, looking up at the stopped clock. It shows 1:51 remains in the game.

Turn the page.

For the Rams, that's too much time. Your defense is tired, and the Rams use every second of that time on a game-winning drive. You hang your head low as they score a touchdown and a two-point conversion. It's a heartbreaking way to lose the Super Bowl. If only you could have used up a little more time.

THE END

To follow another path, turn to page 9.
To learn more about Football, turn to page 101.

Your receiver isn't open yet, and you don't think you can run it in. So you spin to your left and run backward, away from the defenders and the goal line.

One Los Angeles defender launches himself toward you, but you manage to spin out of his grasp. You've got half a second before the next pass rusher arrives. It's just enough time to scan the field.

Your primary receiver isn't open. But another is streaking across the back of the end zone. You can hear the defender's footsteps. He's about to crush you. But you don't flinch. You sling a pass with all your might. The ball sails past the outstretched fingers of a linebacker—right into your receiver's arms.

The defender slams into you. It's the hardest you've ever been hit. You slam to the turf with a sickening crunch. As your team celebrates and the crowd goes nuts, you lie in pain. It's a broken collarbone—you can tell already. The training staff rushes out to treat you even as the celebration spills onto the field.

You're the hero of the game and win the Super Bowl MVP. But you don't get to celebrate with your team. Instead, you watch the coverage on TV from a hospital room. It's not quite the way you pictured winning the big game, but you'll take it.

THE END
To follow another path, turn to page 9.
To learn more about football, turn to page 101.

CHAPTER 5
AN ALL-AMERICAN GAME

Football is one of the most popular sports in North America. But football fans of a century ago would barely recognize the game. In the 1800s, football was more like modern-day rugby or soccer. There were no passing plays—players weren't even allowed to carry the ball. In some versions, there was no limit to the number of players on each side.

The game evolved with time. In the late 1870s, former college athlete Walter Camp wrote a formal rule book for the game. He proposed many of the rules that fans still know today. They included a limit of eleven players on each side and starting each play with a snap from a "line of scrimmage."

As the game took shape, it grew in popularity. Early on, college football ruled. But by the 1900s, professional teams traveled and played around the country. Then in 1920, a group of owners gathered at a car dealership in Canton, Ohio. They formed a new professional football league, the American Professional Football Conference (APFC). Two years later, the APFC changed its name to the National Football League (NFL).

The NFL helped boost the popularity of professional football. By 1960, pro football was big business. That year, a group of business leaders formed the new American Football League (AFL) to compete with the NFL. The rival league battled for the best players and the attention of fans. The NFL remained more popular, but the AFL kept going.

By 1966, it was clear that the AFL would never surpass the NFL. So the two leagues agreed to merge. Part of their agreement was that the champions of the two leagues would face off in a winner-take-all game. It was called the AFL-NFL World Championship Game. But it quickly became known as the Super Bowl. A new era of football had begun.

Over the decades, the Super Bowl became the biggest sporting event in the world. Fans flocked to see the game. Millions watched on TV. Celebrity-filled halftime shows and creative TV commercials made it a pop culture event, even among nonsports fans.

Meanwhile, football thrived at amateur levels as well. For years, high schools have battled for local and state titles. Since the 2014 season, the top teams have faced off in the College Football Playoff National Championship.

In recent years, many fans and players have become worried about the safety of the game. Studies have shown that many retired NFL players suffer from permanent brain damage. The risk of concussions and other brain injuries has led to several rule changes, especially at the amateur levels. Yet football remains, at its core, a violent game.

How will the game change over the next 100 years? Will it still look like the sport that millions of fans know and love? Or will it be as unrecognizable to us as the modern game would be to fans 100 years ago? Only time will tell.

GLOSSARY

blitz (BLITZ)—a play in which defenders who don't normally rush the quarterback do so

checkdown (CHEK-doun)—a short pass thrown as a last resort to a running back or tight end because the wide receivers aren't open

formation (for-MAY-shuhn)—the pattern in which players line up for the start of a play

hard count (HARD KOUNT)—the use of a quarterback's voice to trick the defense into thinking the ball has been snapped

interception (in-tur-SEP-shuhn)—a play in which the defensive team catches a pass

juke (JOOK)—a quick turn or bend to mislead an opponent

option (op-SHUHN)—a play in which a quarterback can choose whether to pass, run, or pitch the ball

rainbow pass (RAYN-boh PASS)—a high-arching pass

screen pass (SKREEN PASS)—when the quarterback fakes a long pass but then throws a short pass to a receiver who is positioned behind a group of blockers

slant route (SLANT ROWT)—when a receiver runs up the field at a 45-degree angle

snap (SNAP)—to pick up the ball off the ground and pass it between the legs back to another player

TEST YOUR FOOTBALL KNOWLEDGE

1. Which is the name of a defensive position?

- A. halfback
- B. cornerback
- C. quarterback

2. Which score is impossible in a football game?

- A. 3-1
- B. 4-3
- C. 76-0

3. Which team won the first Super Bowl?

- A. Kansas City Chiefs
- B. Green Bay Packers
- C. New York Yankees

4. Which is not the name of a passing play?

- A. Hail Mary
- B. flea-flicker
- C. clown car

5. How many points do you have if you score four field goals and a safety?

- A. 5
- B. 14
- C. 15

6. How many players are allowed on the field for each team?

- A. 11
- B. 12
- C. 13

7. Which stat measures tackles of the passer behind the line of scrimmage?

- A. rush
- B. dig
- C. sack

8. Which quarterback has won the most Super Bowls?

- A. Brett Favre
- B. Peyton Manning
- C. Tom Brady

9. When was the first NFL game played?

- A. 1899
- B. 1920
- C. 1938

10. Which two teams have played in the most Super Bowls without ever winning?

- A. Carolina Panthers and Arizona Cardinals
- B. Minnesota Vikings and Buffalo Bills
- C. Cincinnati Bengals and Atlanta Falcons

Answers: 1.B 2.A 3.B 4.C 5.B 6.A 7.C 8.C 9.B 10.B

DISCUSSION QUESTIONS

>>> Who do you think is the greatest football player of all time? Give reasons for your choice.

>>> Some people think football is too violent. Do you agree? Why or why not?

>>> If you could choose between winning the college championship or the Super Bowl, which would you choose? Why?

>>> If you could play in the NFL, which position would you choose? What skills would you need?

AUTHOR BIOGRAPHY

Matt Doeden began his career as a sportswriter, covering everything from high school sports to the NFL. Since then he has written hundreds of children's and young adult books on topics ranging from history to sports to current events. His book *Darkness Everywhere: The Assassination of Mohandas Gandhi* was listed among the Best Children's Books of the Year by the Children's Book Committee at Bank Street College. Doeden lives in Minnesota with his wife and two children.

ILLUSTRATOR BIOGRAPHY

Fran Bueno was born and lives in Santiago de Compostela in Spain. Since he was a little kid, he has loved comic books. He was reading *El Jabato* at age eight, a comic book that his father always bought him, and in that exact moment he decided to become an artist. He studied at art school and will always be grateful to his parents for supporting him. His motivation is to do what he does best and enjoys most. He loves traveling with his wife and kids, being with friends, books, music, movies, and TV shows. Just a regular guy? He would agree.

CHECK OUT ALL 4 BOOKS IN THIS SERIES!

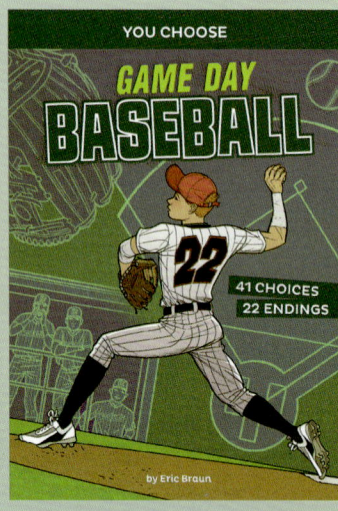

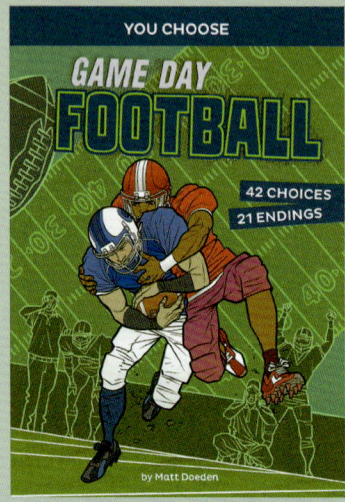

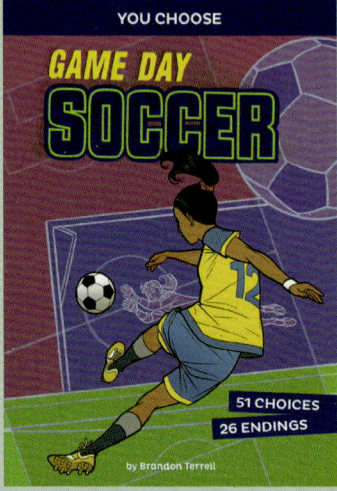

YOU CHOOSE

GAME DAY
BASKETBALL

AN INTERACTIVE SPORTS STORY

BY BRANDON TERRELL
ILLUSTRATED BY FRAN BUENO

CAPSTONE PRESS
a capstone imprint

You Choose Books are published by Capstone Press, an imprint of Capstone.
1710 Roe Crest Drive
North Mankato, Minnesota 56003
www.capstonepub.com

Copyright © 2021 by Capstone Press, a Capstone imprint. All rights reserved. No part of this publication may be reproduced in whole or in part, or stored in a retrieval system, or transmitted in any form or by any means, electronic, mechanical, photocopying, recording, or otherwise, without written permission of the publisher.

Library of Congress Cataloging-in-Publication Data
Names: Terrell, Brandon, 1978- author. | Bueno, Fran, illustrator.
Title: Game day basketball : an interactive sports story / by Brandon Terrell ; [illustrated by Fran Bueno].
Description: North Mankato, Minnesota : Capstone Press, [2021] | Series: You choose: Game day sports | Audience: Ages 8-11. | Audience: Grades 4-6. | Summary: It is the basketball championship game and the reader's choices can mean the difference between a triumphant victory and a heartbreaking loss.
Identifiers: LCCN 2020039273 (print) | LCCN 2020039274 (ebook) | ISBN 9781496696021 (hardcover) | ISBN 9781496697110 (paperback) | ISBN 9781977154262 (ebook pdf)
Subjects: LCSH: Plot-your-own stories. | CYAC: Basketball--Fiction. | Plot-your-own stories.
Classification: LCC PZ7.T273 Gam 2021 (print) | LCC PZ7.T273 (ebook) | DDC [Fic]--dc23
LC record available at https://lccn.loc.gov/2020039273
LC ebook record available at https://lccn.loc.gov/2020039274

Editorial Credits
Editor: Angie Kaelberer; Designer: Kayla Rossow; Media Researcher: Eric Gohl; Premedia Specialist: Katy LaVigne

Printed and bound in China. PO6238

TABLE OF CONTENTS

About Your Game 5

CHAPTER 1
The Edgeview Curse 7

CHAPTER 2
Making the Plays 13

CHAPTER 3
Scoring Machine 51

CHAPTER 4
Playing the Post 79

CHAPTER 5
Hoop Dreams 103

Glossary 106
Test Your Basketball Knowledge 107
Discussion Questions 110
Author Biography 111
Illustrator Biography 111

ABOUT YOUR GAME

YOU are a talented basketball player who has used your skills to help your team reach the championship game. But there's just one problem. Your school has never won the championship, while your opponent has won the title many times in the past. People say your team is cursed when playing this team. Can you put your superstitions aside to help lead your team to victory?

Chapter 1 sets the scene. Then you choose which path to read. Follow the directions at the bottom of the page as you read. The decisions you make will change your outcome. After you finish one path, go back and read the others for new perspectives and more adventures.

CHAPTER 1
THE EDGEVIEW CURSE

"Argh! Where are they?"

Your room is a mess. Books, sports equipment, and clothes are scattered around the floor. You lift a pair of sweatpants to look underneath them. No luck.

Your dad appears in your doorway. "Are you ready to go?" he asks.

You shake your head. "I need my lucky socks," you tell him.

"Those stinky old things?" he asks. "They're in the laundry room."

Turn the page.

You dash down the stairs. Your older brother, Nick, is at the bottom, and you nearly crash into him. "Whoa!" he says, spinning in a circle. "Save that speed for the court, bro!"

You ignore him, hurrying into the laundry room. Stacks of clean clothes sit on a table. Are your lucky socks among them? You hope not. You're crazy superstitious, and you haven't washed them since your basketball team went on a winning streak. Today is the championship game, and if the luck has been washed from your socks, you don't know what will happen.

You spy a hint of white with two green stripes poking out from the dirty clothes on the floor.

You sigh with relief, pluck the dirty socks from the pile, and slip them on your bare feet. You wiggle your toes. "Perfect."

Your family piles into the car. You sit with Nick in the back seat.

"So," he says, "are you nervous about the Edgeview Curse?"

You stare at Nick. How could he bring up the curse now?

The Edgeview Middle School Tigers have never won a championship before. They've made it to the big game—Nick was on the team two of those times—but they've never won.

"We're on a hot streak," you tell him. "I think we've got a great chance."

Nick sighs and looks out his window. "Yeah," he says. "I remember thinking that too."

At school, you walk past the trophy case on your way to the locker room. It's filled with second-place and participation trophies. They're constant reminders of the school's history.

To make matters worse, today you'll face the same team Nick lost to when he played. The same team that's won the championship too many times to count—the Haverford Vipers.

Most of your teammates are already in the locker room. Speedy Saddiq Omar. Liu Zhang, the team's assist leader. The tall Duncan "Dunc" Greene. And Charlie Peretti, the most superstitious of all. Just like you, he's wearing a lucky pair of dirty socks. He's doing the same routine he's done before every game—chewing gum with his earbuds in, listening to music. Coach Willis is there too.

"OK, team," he says. Charlie pops out his earbuds. You lace up your sneakers. "Here's the starting lineup."

To play point guard and lead the team, turn to page 13.

To show off your jump shot at small forward, turn to page 51.

To take it to the paint and play center, turn to page 79.

CHAPTER 2

MAKING THE PLAYS

The Tigers are on a roll, and part of the reason is that you've taken charge, leading the way as the team's starting point guard. And you're ready to do it again.

Coach Willis leads the way onto the court. The crowd in the gymnasium is electric. You've experienced big crowds this season. But tonight is more than you expected.

You jog onto the court and take your position. At center, Dunc prepares for the tip-off. You see the Viper point guard, Miles Ortega. He's one of the best players in the state.

The ref blows the whistle, and Dunc leaps up for the tip-off. The Viper center flips it back to Miles, who hurries the ball up the court.

Turn the page.

It's clear the Vipers are playing with an intensity you haven't experienced before. They're fast. Miles passes the ball off to another Viper, who easily drains a jump shot.

The quick, easy score makes you feel uncomfortable. This style of play isn't what led you to the championship. From the sidelines, Coach Willis shouts, "Settle down! Get into a rhythm!"

You get the ball and dribble up the court. The game hinges on how you want to play it. It's time to decide.

> To slow down the game, go to page 15.
> To keep pace with the Vipers, turn to page 26.

Coach Willis is right. The Tigers made it here playing in their own style. There's no way you're going to change that now.

You take a deep breath, steady yourself, and bring the ball up the court. When you reach the top of the key, you see Miles crouching low, watching you intently. You shout out your favorite play, "Tiger Roar," and your team moves with skill. As they spread out, you spy Liu open on your left. You quickly feed him the ball. He dishes it to Dunc in the lane. Dunc turns and makes an easy layup.

"Yes!" you shout, pumping your fist.

Your slow play doesn't change the way the Vipers are playing. Miles rushes the ball up the court and feeds the ball to his small forward, Brent Reilly.

Turn the page.

Brent sweeps past Charlie, who was barely able to make it back on defense. Brent makes an easy layup, giving the Vipers the lead again.

The game continues this way. Each time you try to slow down the game, the Vipers speed it back up. They're relentless. And playing to their level is wearing down your team.

As you bring the ball up the court again, you have another chance to slow things down. You'll call an easy play, something that you've run a million times before.

To run a motion offense, go to page 17.
To run a give-and-go offense, turn to page 20.

You hold up your right hand in a peace sign, the signal for motion offense. By running it, you're showing the team they need to treat this game just like any other.

Liu sweeps beneath the hoop, moving from right to left. As he does, Dunc plants himself in front of Liu's defender. You bounce the ball to an open Liu in the corner. He puts up a three-pointer and drains it!

The Tigers go on a run, scoring each time down the court and denying the Vipers.

Near the end of the first half, you're ahead by double digits. You dribble down the court. Miles drapes himself all over you, making it hard to drive or pass the ball. But you have to do something.

> To pass the ball to a teammate, turn to page 18.
> To keep the ball and take the shot, turn to page 19.

If you can dribble past Miles, you'll have a clear lane to the hoop. But then you see two Viper defenders close the gap and realize your chances of making a shot are slim.

Charlie is open, so you dish the ball off to him. But Miles swats it away, and another Viper scoops it up.

"Time-out!" Miles makes a T with his hands, and the ref blows the whistle.

Time is running out in the first half. And after the time-out, Miles leads the Vipers on a roaring comeback. By the time the buzzer sounds, your lead is slim.

Turn to page 38.

You know you can get past Miles. And with a quick step-slide to your left, you breeze by him. But as you do, two Viper defenders close the hole you're driving down. They plant their feet, standing straight up and raising their arms high.

As you go in for the left-handed layup, your hip connects with a Viper defender. He falls to the floor.

Tweep!

The ref stops play. "Foul, offense!" he shouts, pointing at you. "Charging!"

He jogs to the sideline, where the Vipers are set to inbound the ball.

Turn to page 22.

Motion offense is a basic, standard play. Miles and the Vipers may be expecting that. Instead, you quickly perform a crossover dribble and dish the ball to Dunc, who's raced up to the free-throw line.

Miles turns to double-team Dunc, and you race toward the hoop. Dunc flips the ball over his shoulder . . . right into your hands!

You leap, laying the ball on the backboard and sinking the shot.

Miles is furious that you tricked him. When he gets the ball again, he hurries it down the court, pulling up and shooting a three-pointer.

The Viper defenders switch to a full-court press. They're doing all they can to get back into the game. And it's working. You can't seem to get the ball up the court. Their aggressive play infuriates you.

You're frustrated, and as Miles brings the ball up the court, you reach in and swat at the ball.

The ref blows the whistle. "Reaching foul!" he says, pointing at you. The Vipers get the ball on the sideline for an inbound pass.

Turn the page.

Brent, the Viper forward, passes the ball in to Miles. He races up the court.

You crouch low, shuffling your feet and keeping pace with Miles on defense. You're not going to let him get past you.

"Oof!" It feels like you've run into a wall. In fact, the Viper center, Damian Osgood, has set a pick on you. Miles scurries past.

"Switch!" you yell to Dunc, who was defending the center. He should be taking Miles, but he's caught up on the far side of the court. That leaves you to defend both Miles and Damian!

They both move toward the hoop.

> To dart over and cover Miles, go to page 23.
> To stick with covering the center, turn to page 24.

I have to cover Miles, you think. *He's my responsibility.*

But as you dash over, Damian's arm lashes out and strikes you in the chest. You bend over, both hands on your knees. The ref calls a foul on Damian.

"Come on out!" Coach Willis says, waving you to the sidelines.

You slump into a chair. "Hudson! You're in!" Coach says. Hudson Hart, a lean bench player, hustles onto the court.

"You okay?" Coach asks. You nod.

As you sit, the Vipers go on a scoring streak. You're itching to get back into the game.

That will have to wait until the second half. As the buzzer sounds for halftime, the Tigers hold a slim three-point lead over the Vipers.

Turn to page 38.

"Switch!" you call again, just to be sure Dunc heard you.

He did, and he hurries over to cover Miles as the Viper point guard breaks down the lane.

That leaves you to cover Damian, who's about a foot taller than you. You're outmatched but doing your best.

Miles pulls up before he reaches Dunc and arcs a fadeaway jump shot at the hoop. It misses, clanging off the rim and heading right toward you and Damian!

Damian nabs the ball out of the air. He quickly puts up a shot. You jump up and swat at the ball, accidentally hitting Damian in the arm instead.

Tweep!

The ref calls you for the shooting foul.

"Shooting two!" the ref adds as everyone lines up for the free throws.

Damian goes to the line. He dribbles twice, exhales, and spins the ball. Then he puts up the first free throw.

Swish!

He does the same for the second shot.

The momentum has swung in the Vipers' favor. As the final minutes of the first half tick away, they come roaring back. By the time the buzzer sounds at the half, the Tigers are holding the slimmest of leads.

Turn to page 38.

You've reached the championship game by playing your style of basketball. Calm, cool, and collected. But if you want to break the curse and keep pace with the Vipers, you're going to need to do more than that. You've heard people talk about playing up to your opponent's level. That's what you need to do.

You hurry down the court, trying to catch the Vipers unprepared. As the Tigers scramble to get into position, you push the ball down the lane, dribbling quickly.

Miles is ready for you. He swats the ball from your hand. It careens away, landing in the hands of the Viper center, Damian Osgood.

The Vipers take the ball down the court, quickly scoring again.

"Slow it down!" Coach Willis urges from the bench.

You don't, though. The next time down the court, you quickly dish the ball to Dunc under the hoop. He hooks a shot off the backboard and into the basket.

Turn the page.

The Vipers aren't slowing down. As the first half continues, you find yourself racing from one end of the court to the other.

And Miles doesn't seem to be slowing down. You gasp as you hurry down the court after him. He dribbles to the top of the key before you can reach him. He feeds the ball to Damian, who arcs the ball back out to the Viper small forward. He drains an easy jump shot.

You're winded, and part of you hopes Coach Willis will call a time-out. But he doesn't. He's anxiously pacing the sideline.

The next time the Vipers have the ball, you consider calling a time-out yourself. Or maybe asking a teammate to switch defensive positions with you. You're afraid you won't be able to handle Miles much longer.

To continue playing defense on Miles, go to page 29.
To ask a teammate to switch, turn to page 33.

No, you think. Miles is my responsibility. I've got this.

And so you keep playing defense on Miles. As he brings the ball up the court, you dig down to find more strength. Take a deep breath. Steady yourself.

Miles fakes right, then dribbles between his legs and breaks to the left. You stumble but are able to follow him. He goes to dish the ball, pulling up and clutching the ball in both hands. You drape yourself all over him, not letting him get the pass off.

Miles throws out his elbows, waving them back and forth.

Another Viper races up behind him, and Miles is able to get past your defense, feeding the ball to him.

The Viper player puts up the shot and misses!

Turn the page.

Damian gets the rebound, and Miles slips around you. He's caught you completely off guard. If you weren't so tired, you would have stayed with him.

Damian fakes a shot, then bounces the ball back to Miles. You're trailing him as he slips down the lane toward the hoop.

You've got a bead on the ball, but it may be best to just foul Miles before he shoots.

> To go for the ball, go to page 31.
> To try to foul Miles, turn to page 43.

Miles dashes down the lane. He's quick, but maybe that's not an advantage. You notice his dribbling is sloppy.

I don't need to foul him, you think. *I'll just go for the ball.* You dart your arm around his left side, being sure not to touch him as you swat at the ball.

You miss! But your action has thrown Miles off his rhythm. He goes up for the layup, but the ball bricks off the bottom of the rim.

Charlie comes down with the rebound. You stumble, falling to one knee as Charlie looks to pass the ball to you. Instead, he brings it up the court.

The Tigers are still playing with the same intensity as the Vipers. As Charlie reaches midcourt, he sees Dunc open under the hoop. He passes the ball hard and fast to the center, who spins and slides a perfectly arced shot off his fingertips.

Turn the page.

The ball drops in.

This change in momentum is enough to propel the Tigers into the lead. When the buzzer sounds at halftime, you're ahead of the Vipers by six points.

Turn to page 38.

You suck in a deep breath, the air stinging your lungs. Miles has run you ragged the whole first quarter. You're afraid he'll take advantage of your tiredness as the game continues.

"Hey, Saddiq," you say, getting the other guard's attention. The Viper he's defending, a kid named Eliot Musgrave, isn't as fast as Miles. Saddiq doesn't look nearly as tired as you. "Can we switch it up?"

Saddiq looks at Miles, then back at you. He nods. "Sure thing," he says, hurrying over to the Viper point guard.

The switch is just what you needed. Defending Eliot is enough to regain your energy, while Saddiq is able to keep Miles to only a single bucket.

Turn the page.

As you jog onto the court for the start of the second quarter, you sidle up to Saddiq. "Switch back?" you ask.

He bumps your fist. "Got it."

You hustle over to Miles. "Miss me?" you ask him as Damian inbounds the pass to Miles. You quickly steal it midair and hurry down the court.

You pull up at the free-throw line and put up a jump shot. It rattles around the rim and falls through.

The end of the first half looms, and the score is close.

"Time-out!" Coach Willis calls. The ref blows the whistle, and you all jog over.

"Huddle up," the coach says. He kneels in the center of the huddle, scribbling on his clipboard. "Here's the play we're going to run."

He draws it out quickly, and you can see the confused looks on the other players' faces. It's a play you've never run.

The whistle sounds again, and you have to hurry back onto the court. Charlie inbounds the ball to you, and you slow down the game.

Coach nods at you to run the play. But then you recall the confused looks in the huddle. Besides, Liu is open in the corner, and he's your best three-point shooter.

> To run the coach's confusing play, turn to page 36.
> To pass the ball to an open Liu, turn to page 46.

Sure, the play is confusing. But you trust Coach Willis. When he gives you a play to run, you run it. So even though Liu is open in the corner, you stop at the top of the key and call for the play.

The guys run the play surprisingly well! Charlie and Liu cross under the hoop, while Dunc runs up to the line. That clears the area under the hoop, and Saddiq breaks for it. You lob the ball up over Dunc and right into Saddiq's hands. The defenders rush in, leaving Charlie and Liu open in the corner.

Saddiq dishes the ball out to Charlie, who puts up the three-pointer.

"Nothin' but net!" Charlie says as the ball drops in.

You look up at the clock. There's less than a minute left in the half, and Charlie's shot has broken a tie and given you a lead.

Miles hustles the ball up the court, but the Vipers are unable to score.

Bzzzzzttt!

The first half is over, and the Tigers hold a slim lead. If you're going to win, you're going to need a strong second half.

Turn the page.

"All right, guys!" Coach Willis says. "We had some great moments in the first half. A few setbacks here and there, but you've made it this far. I want that same level of intensity in the second half. We do that, and this dumb curse will be a thing of the past."

At the mention of the Edgeview Curse, you see a couple of guys squirm. Charlie adjusts his lucky socks.

You do the same.

Once you're back on the court, however, all that fades away. Or so you think. When Saddiq passes the ball to Charlie and Charlie shoots, the ball misses the hoop entirely.

"Nice air ball," Miles says, snickering as the Vipers get the rebound.

Turn the page.

A minute later, Charlie is fouled while shooting a fadeaway jumper. When he goes to the line, he bricks both free throws.

Something's up, you think as you jog over to him. "Calm down," you tell him. "Just relax, and you'll be fine."

But do you believe your own words? The next time you bring the ball up the court, you notice the Vipers are leaving Charlie wide open. They don't believe he can make a shot.

Do you?

> To pass the ball to Charlie, go to page 41.
> To find another open Tiger, turn to page 47.

Sure, Charlie has missed a few shots. And he's likely letting his superstition get the better of him. But he's a great player, and the fact that the Vipers are leaving him wide open is ridiculous.

You quickly feed him the ball. His eyes grow wide as the ball comes his way. But then he sees the wide-open three-pointer he has in front of him. He pivots, aims, and puts up the shot.

Swish!

"Yes!" you shout. "Great shot, Charlie!"

Charlie smiles. He bends down and adjusts his lucky socks. Then he points at you and says, "I'm back!"

Turn the page.

Charlie's three is the momentum shift the Tigers need to start the second half. As time ticks on, the game stays in your favor. But that doesn't mean the Vipers aren't giving you a run for your money.

Near the end of the fourth quarter, the Vipers take a one-point lead, their first of the game.

"Time-out!" Coach calls.

The team huddles, and you look out into the crowd. You see Nick, and it makes you think about the curse. When the huddle breaks, you realize you didn't hear the coach's play call.

The inbound pass comes your way. But you have no idea what to do. Liu and Dunc are both open. Seconds tick away.

> To pass the ball to Dunc, turn to page 48.
> To pass the ball to Liu, turn to page 49.

Miles is on his way to making an easy layup. But you remember Coach Willis telling you at practice earlier in the week that Miles is iffy at the free-throw line. You make a quick decision.

Miles is about to go up for the shot, raising his right arm with the ball. You slide your left arm around his chest to foul him before he can shoot. But he gets the shot off, the ball arcing toward the hoop. Even worse, he stumbles after he shoots. The two of you, tangled together, fall to a heap on the court floor.

From the floor, you watch as the ball rattles around the rim and drops in.

Tweep! The ref blows his whistle and points at you. Miles is going to the free-throw line for an extra shot.

Turn the page.

But something else worries you more. The pain in your arm is intense. You curl your fingers into a fist and cringe.

Coach Willis jogs over. "You OK?" he asks.

You shake your head. You know the curse has gotten the best of you. You'll be riding the bench the rest of the game.

You can only watch as the Vipers score an easy victory.

THE END

To follow another path, turn to page 11.
To learn more about basketball, turn to page 103.

An open Liu is too good to pass up. You quickly dish him the ball, and he puts up the shot.

It bricks off the rim.

Dunc and Damian both go for the rebound and collide. Dunc steps on Damian's ankle, and his own ankle twists sharply.

"Ahh!" Dunc falls to the court.

It's clear Dunc will need to ice it, and he's unlikely to return to the game. Saddiq helps Dunc out. Then you see Coach glaring at you.

"Hudson, you're in," Coach says. You sit on the bench.

"I told you to run the play," Coach Willis says. You're still on the bench when the Vipers pull away to win the championship.

THE END
To follow another path, turn to page 11.
To learn more about basketball, turn to page 103.

Charlie sees you looking his way, but then you spy Dunc with his hand up and feed him the ball instead. Dunc turns and drains the easy shot.

"Nice one!" You bump fists with Dunc as you jog down the court.

The Tigers never let up and soar into the fourth quarter with a commanding lead. It looks like you're going to break the jinx. And when the final buzzer sounds, you celebrate an amazing victory!

But you look over and see Charlie sulking. He didn't score in the second half. When you really think about it, you don't even recall him getting the ball.

Sure, you won. But you did it at the cost of your teammate's pride and confidence. That kind of victory feels pretty hollow.

THE END

To follow another path, turn to page 11.
To learn more about basketball, turn to page 103.

Dunc is elbowing with Damian Osgood, the Viper center. But he's ready for the pass. You rocket the ball down to him with seconds left. Dunc takes it, spins, and puts up the shot.

Clang! He misses! But then . . .

Tweep! "Foul on the Vipers!" the ref shouts, pointing to Damian.

Dunc goes to the line. If he makes both shots, you'll win. When Dunc misses the first shot, you whisper to him, "You got this. Make it and we'll go to OT."

You cross your fingers. But then you hear Dunc whisper, "We're cursed." And sure enough, he misses the second free throw.

You've lost the game.

THE END
To follow another path, turn to page 11.
To learn more about basketball, turn to page 103.

Time is running out. Dunc is in the paint, throwing elbows. And Miles is shadowing you closely. So when you see Liu get open on the right side of the court, you quickly feed him the ball.

He doesn't have a great shot, but there's no time. He puts up a jump shot that arcs through the air.

Nothing but net!

The buzzer sounds, and the Tigers race onto the court to celebrate. Coach Willis bellows, "We've done it! We've broken the Edgeview Curse!"

A first-place trophy will finally find its place in the school's trophy case!

THE END
To follow another path, turn to page 11.
To learn more about basketball, turn to page 103.

CHAPTER 3

SCORING MACHINE

Your jump shot is the best on the team. You and Nick have been practicing it at home all season. So when Coach Willis says you're starting at small forward, you're not surprised. Your shooting skills and speed are perfect for the position.

"All right, guys," Coach Willis says. "Let's go out and win a championship!"

The crowd waiting for you in the gym is electric. It's the biggest crowd you've had all season. Many of them are clearly curious to see if you have what it takes to break the Edgeview Curse.

Dunc lines up against the Viper center, Damian Osgood, for the tip-off. The ref tosses the ball high. Dunc is able to swat it first, sending it in Saddiq's direction.

Turn the page.

Saddiq, at point guard, brings the ball up the court. You line up to his left, break for the hoop, then stop and come back out. He feeds you the ball, and you go for a shot. Your confidence builds as you score the first points of the game.

The Vipers are fast and intense, though. Their point guard, Miles Ortega, is the best player in the league. Saddiq is having a tough time guarding him. The Vipers lead the game for most of the first half.

You need to change that. Fast.

As Saddiq brings the ball up the court, you flash out to the key, setting a pick on Miles and giving Saddiq a chance to drive. You spin, opening up and finding yourself alone at the top of the key. Saddiq sees you and dishes you the ball. But a defender is coming up fast to guard you.

To pass to an open Dunc, go to page 53.
To take the shot yourself, turn to page 55.

Dunc is in the paint, boxing out Damian and getting himself open. You fake a jump shot, sending the Viper defender off his feet. With the defender off-balance, you rocket a bounce pass around him, right into Dunc's hands.

Dunc, still battling with Damian, spins to put up the shot. But Damian juts out an elbow and unintentionally clips Dunc in the chin.

Dunc lets go of the ball and bends over, stunned and hurt.

Tweep!

"Foul on the Vipers!" the ref calls out, pointing to Damian.

Dazed, Dunc goes to the foul line. He misses both free throws.

Turn the page.

Coach Willis pulls Dunc out for the rest of the first half. You can feel the change in momentum without Dunc. The Vipers take full advantage. When the buzzer sounds at the end of the first half, they have a commanding lead.

Dunc steps out onto the court to start the second half. "I'm not going to let that curse stop me," he says, rubbing his chin.

And it seems like he's right. You pull close to the Vipers in the second half.

With seconds left on the clock, Dunc has the ball in the paint. He goes up for the shot, and it bricks off the rim.

It's heading in your direction!

To go after the rebound, turn to page 67.
To see where the ball comes down, turn to page 68.

Dunc is open. A Viper defender is racing to cover you. But your team needs a spark. And you're a step away from being behind the three-point line.

You step back, raising the ball to shoot. But you pump-fake, and the Viper falls for it. He leaps into the air to swat the shot away and sails right past you, leaving you with an open shot.

Nothing but net.

"Nice shot!" Coach Willis shouts from the sidelines. You can barely hear him over the roar of the crowd.

You sense a change in the air. The momentum has shifted in the Tigers' favor.

Turn the page.

The next time down the court, you sink another jumper. Then a third. You're on a roll! The Tigers are back in the game, and it's all thanks to you! You're carrying the team.

As you jog back on defense, though, you see Charlie and Liu whispering to one another. Charlie throws a nasty glance in your direction. They can't possibly be upset about your shooting streak, can they?

After Damian sinks a hook shot for the Vipers, keeping their lead narrow, Saddiq brings the ball to midcourt. Liu is on the left side alongside you. Saddiq passes the ball your way, but it's knocked away by a Viper.

You and Liu both have a shot at grabbing it before it goes out-of-bounds.

> To let Liu go after the ball, go to page 57.
> To go after the ball, turn to page 69.

You've got a shot at the ball, but so does Liu. Your mind flashes back to the looks your teammates were giving you.

You stop in your tracks. Liu snags the ball cleanly, quickly passing it to Charlie in the corner. Charlie is covered, though, and he passes it to you.

In an effort to gain back your team's respect, you quickly pass the ball over to Saddiq. Saddiq takes the shot.

Swish! He makes it!

By the time the buzzer sounds at the half, the Tigers have clawed their way back into the game.

"Great job, guys!" Coach Willis says in the locker room at halftime. "Remember, teamwork is what's gonna help us win this game. Got it?"
The team responds with a loud, "Yes, sir!"

Turn the page.

"This curse everyone's thinking about?" Coach Willis continues. "It means nothing. And if you continue to work together, you'll prove it."

"We can do this, guys!" you blurt out. The team looks your way. Smiles cross their faces. They're starting to believe.

The second half starts strong. Charlie sinks a pair of three-pointers, tugging on his lucky socks after each one. Saddiq leads with confidence. And you show off your jump shot.

Miles and the Vipers are beyond frustrated. The Tigers are almost in the lead.

After a missed shot by Damian, Dunc gets the rebound and passes it to you. You hurry the ball down the court. Charlie is keeping pace with you, but so is Miles. It's a two-on-one fast break!

To fake the pass and take it yourself, turn to page 60.
To pass the fast break off to Charlie, turn to page 70.

You've been dishing the ball off most of the second half and assume that's what Miles thinks you'll do now too. So instead of passing the ball to Charlie, who has a bad angle at the hoop, you fake the pass. Miles bites, stepping back and giving you extra room to drive to the hoop.

You put up the shot and feel Miles swiping you on the wrist. The ball rattles around the rim and falls in.

Tweep!

"Foul!" the ref shouts. "One free throw!"

You have a shot at making it a three-point play!

You toe the free-throw line and take a deep breath. You spin the ball in your hands, then dribble once. Twice. Set. And shoot.

Swish!

With that play, the Tigers have taken the lead!

You hold on to that lead as the game nears its end. But then the Vipers land a three-pointer, followed by a turnover and an easy layup. Suddenly you're down two points with seconds to go!

Saddiq brings the ball down the court. He passes off to you. You can feel the seconds ticking away. What do you do? Dunc is fighting it out with Damian in the paint. And you don't have the best shot.

But there's Saddiq, open at the top of the key, behind the three-point line.

To pass back to Saddiq, who is open for the three-pointer, turn to page 62.

To pass the ball to Dunc for a two-pointer, turn to page 72.

You quickly feed Saddiq the ball, and he puts up the shot.

The world moves in slow motion. The ball arcs high. You hold your breath. The ball hits the front of the rim, bounces back, ricochets off the backboard, and drops through the hoop.

BZZZZZZTTT!

Time expires, and Saddiq's three-pointer wins the game!

Tweep!

The ref's whistle stops the celebration short.

"What's going on?" you ask.

The ref points at Saddiq's left foot. His toe is over the three-point line. "On the line," the ref explains. "Sorry, but the shot only counts for two points, not three."

Your heart sinks. There's confusion in the stands as Tigers fans try to figure out what's happening. But then the referee makes it clear by blowing his whistle again and shouting, "Overtime!"

Coach Willis huddles you together. "OK, guys," he says. He has to talk loud to be heard over the crowd. The whole gym must be able to feel that the curse could end today, as they're cheering louder than ever. "Take a deep breath and relax. You're tired, I get that. But now's the time to dig down and find that extra bit of strength."

"Let's go, Tigers!" you shout.

"Tigers . . . ROAR!" the whole team replies.

You take the court, glancing at your teammates. They may sound fired up, but they look exhausted. Fortunately, the Vipers look the same.

Turn the page.

The Vipers get the tip-off, and Miles takes the ball down for an easy score. They may look tired, but they're definitely not playing that way.

Overtime is a battle. The Tigers try to keep pace with the Vipers, but it's hard. Saddiq makes a pass that's stolen, and Dunc has an easy shot blocked by Damian.

Still, Charlie sinks a three-pointer, and you contribute a pair of fadeaway jumpers. You're keeping the game close, but time is running out, and the Tigers are down by two points.

The Vipers get the ball back, and Coach Willis instructs you to foul Damian and send him to the free-throw line. But you've got four fouls, which means you're one foul away from being out of the game.

To let Damian bring the ball up the court, turn to page 66.
To foul Damian, turn to page 74.

You've got one foul left, but you don't want to use it. Still, that's what Coach Willis asked you to do.

However, as Damian gets the ball, it's almost like he can sense the foul coming. Instead, you only pretend like you're going to reach in for the foul.

Your fake works!

Damian accidentally dribbles the ball off his foot. As the ball is about to go out-of-bounds, Charlie scoops it up. He dishes it back to you. You glance at the clock. Seconds left. Dunc is open down in the lane.

To pass the ball to Dunc, turn to page 76.
To take the last-second shot yourself, turn to page 77.

You're down by only a few points. You need the rebound to keep pace with the Vipers. So you leap for the ball as it arcs through the air in your direction.

Miles has the same idea. The two of you collide in midair, but Miles snags the ball. You fall to the court, rolling out-of-bounds. From the floor, you watch Miles pass the ball up to Damian, who breaks for the hoop. The Tigers are shorthanded as you stagger to your feet, and the Vipers easily score, extending their lead. The Tigers can't make any points as the seconds run out on the clock.

The Edgeview Curse strikes again!

THE END

To follow another path, turn to page 11.
To learn more about basketball, turn to page 103.

You're about to leap for the rebound, but hesitate. Miles is also heading for the ball. If you jump now, you'll likely collide with him.

But you're ready. When Miles comes down with the ball, you're there to swat it from his hands.

"I'll take that!" you say as you grab the ball.

You quickly pass to Charlie, who puts up a three-pointer.

Swish!

"Yes!" You bump fists with Charlie. His three turns the tide of the game, and before long, he's drained two more, and the Tigers have pulled ahead.

When the final buzzer sounds, you and your teammates have broken the curse!

THE END

To follow another path, turn to page 11.
To learn more about basketball, turn to page 103.

You've got a great shot at retrieving the ball, and you're not going to let anyone else grab it.

You dive for the ball and accidentally strike Liu! He's swept off his feet, landing hard on the court. He cries out and clutches his right knee.

Oh no, you think. *I've just injured my friend!*

You go to help Liu. He swats your hand away. "Ball hog," he mutters.

It feels like there's a brick in your stomach. You watch as Charlie helps Liu off the court. Coach Willis comes out and helps.

The rest of the Tigers angrily look your way. Your greediness has cost you a player and the respect of the team. It's no surprise when the Tigers lose the game.

THE END
To follow another path, turn to page 11.
To learn more about basketball, turn to page 103.

Charlie is on your left, and he's not good at left-handed layups. But Miles is closer to you than Charlie is. So you swing the ball around your back and pass it perfectly over to Charlie.

Charlie goes for the layup. But he has a bad angle, and the ball strikes the bottom of the rim. It ricochets right into Miles's hands.

Miles laughs. "Nice shot," he says, dishing the ball ahead to midcourt.

The Viper at midcourt races forward. Even this deep into the game, the Vipers are playing fast and aggressive. Your defense isn't ready for it, and Damian is able to get the ball and sink an easy hoop.

"Stupid socks," you hear Charlie mutter behind you. You nod.

The lucky socks aren't the only thing not working. The shift in momentum is affecting your entire team. Air balls. Steals. Easy shots missed.

Nothing is going in your favor.

With all that goes wrong in the second half, the curse feels more real than ever. The Vipers continue to expand their lead, and there's nothing you can do to change that. You lose the game by 10 points.

THE END
To follow another path, turn to page 11.
To learn more about basketball, turn to page 103.

You're down two points. One easy shot ties the game and sends it to overtime. It's an easy decision.

You pass the ball down to Dunc. He pivots, jumps, and banks an easy shot off the backboard.

Tie game! But there are still several seconds left. "Time-out!" the Viper coach yells.

You jog over to the sideline. Coach Willis is chewing his fingernails.

"We left too much time on the clock," he says. "So play safe. No fouls! Do you hear me?"

The team nods.

The Vipers get the inbound pass on their side of the court. They line up, and the Tigers stay close. "Tough D," you remind your teammates.

The Viper making the inbound pass has Damian in his sights. When the play begins, the large center has two players setting picks to get him open. "Watch the big guy!" you shout.

But then the Viper arcs the ball high across the court to a wide-open Miles!

"No!" In the rush to cover Damian, you've forgotten all about Miles. The Viper point guard gets the ball, dribbles forward, and with one second left on the clock, sinks an easy jumper.

It's over. You can only hang your head as the Vipers celebrate on the court.

THE END

To follow another path, turn to page 11.
To learn more about basketball, turn to page 103.

Coach Willis once again shouts, "Foul him!" By sending Damian to the free-throw line, you're taking a gamble that he'll miss one or both of the shots, giving you another chance to tie or win the game.

As Damian gets the ball, and before he can pass the ball off to another player, you reach in and swat at the ball, hitting Damian in the chest as you do.

Tweep!

"Foul!" The ref points at you, and your shoulders slump. "That's five!"

You've officially fouled out of the game. You jog to the bench. Coach Willis slaps you on the back. "I know it's hard," he says, "but you did the right thing." Hudson Hart takes your place.

It's a gamble, having Damian go to the line. And when he sinks the first shot, your stomach drops. He's locked in and focused. There's no way he's going to miss.

Sure enough, Damian makes the second shot. The Tigers fans are quiet.

When Miles steals the ball from Saddiq during the next possession, you lose hope. The Tigers lose in overtime, and you can only watch from the bench.

THE END
To follow another path, turn to page 11.
To learn more about basketball, turn to page 103.

Dunc is fighting it out with Damian in the lane, but finds a way to get open. A simple shot from the tall center is all you need to tie this game and have a chance to break the curse!

You quickly pass the ball down to him, but Damian lashes out an arm and knocks the ball away from Dunc.

Miles scoops up the loose ball.

"Foul him!" Coach Willis bellows.

But Miles is too speedy, and as the clock runs out, he's still flitting around the court with the ball.

The curse strikes again!

THE END

To follow another path, turn to page 11.
To learn more about basketball, turn to page 103.

There are only a few ticks of the clock left. It seems like you can feel each one through your body.

You look down the lane at Dunc. Maybe you can sneak a pass to him. But it's a gamble. Your Viper defender sees your eyes, though, and moves down into the lane, freeing you up for a three-point shot.

00:03 ... 00:02 ... 00:01 ...

You put up the shot.

BZZZZZTT!

The whole gym waits with bated breath. The ball soars through the air.

Swish!

"Yes!" You leap into the air, pumping your fist. You did it! The Tigers have broken the curse!

THE END
To follow another path, turn to page 11.
To learn more about basketball, turn to page 103.

CHAPTER 4
PLAYING THE POST

"Are you ready for the tip-off?" Coach Willis says to you. It sounds like you'll be playing center for the Tigers today. You're cool with that. Center isn't typically your position, but if that's where Coach Willis wants you to play, that's where you'll play.

You step onto the court alongside your teammates. A ref stands at center court with the ball, ready for the tip-off.

The Viper center, Damian Osgood, is taller than you. But you've got a strong vertical and can jump pretty high.

The ref blows the whistle. You leap and swat the ball back to Saddiq, who's playing point guard.

Turn the page.

Saddiq brings the ball up the court. You head down into the paint.

"Lucky break, squirt," Damian mutters, commenting on your size difference. You try to get open, but can already sense he's going to play aggressively. If you're going to break the curse, you're going to have to do the same.

Saddiq passes the ball to Charlie. You pivot, driving your hip into Damian to block him out. Charlie bounces the ball to you.

You spin, driving an elbow into Damian's gut as you go up for the shot. He's draped all over you, and the ref calls him for a foul.

"Hey!" Damian shouts. "He hit me!"

You line up for the free throws. Breathe deeply. Spin the ball in your hands. Shoot.

Swish!

The second shot also goes in, giving the Tigers the first points of the game.

As you jog down the court, you spy Damian glaring at you.

The Viper point guard, Miles Ortega, is the best player you've ever faced. He quickly dribbles down the court, dishing a no-look pass to a scrappy forward named Brent.

Brent sinks a jump shot.

Saddiq hurries the ball up the court. You're playing fast and aggressively, just like the Vipers. He passes to Charlie, who shoots. The ball ricochets off the rim, and you box out Damian, going for the rebound.

Saddiq lunges for it too.

> To let Saddiq get the rebound, turn to page 82.
> To go after the rebound, turn to page 91.

The way you and Damian have been grappling, it's better if you both don't dive after the ball. If you do, there's a good chance you'll foul him or one of you will get injured.

You pull up and let Saddiq go after the ball. He's got a better chance.

Saddiq doesn't reach the ball in time, though. It bounces out-of-bounds. "Viper ball!" the ref says.

Miles takes the inbound pass, leading his team down to score. The remainder of the first half goes like that. Every time the Tigers feel like they're climbing back into the game, the Vipers go on a scoring run.

When the buzzer sounds at the half, the Vipers have a commanding lead.

Coach Willis paces the locker room. "We're still in this," he says, but without much conviction. "You just have to believe."

You look around. The guys are tired and sweaty. They don't look like believers. Charlie is tugging at his lucky socks. Saddiq is hanging his head. The curse is weighing heavy in the locker room. You can feel it thick in the air.

"All right, let's go, team!" Coach Willis claps loudly. He's trying his best to get everyone hyped. It's not working.

You wonder if maybe you need to shake things up. You consider pulling Coach aside and talking to him about changing positions.

To talk with Coach Willis, turn to page 84.
To keep quiet, turn to page 87.

"Coach?"

Coach Willis turns at the door of the locker room. The other players have already walked out to shoot warm-ups for the second half. "What's up?" Coach asks.

"I'm getting beat down in the paint," you admit. "And I think Dunc would be better at center than me."

Coach Willis thinks a moment, then nods. "I appreciate your honesty," he says. "Why don't we give it a shot?"

Together, you walk out onto the court. The team is already shooting around, warming up. Coach speaks to Dunc, who looks over at you and nods.

When the second half starts, you're now playing shooting guard alongside Saddiq. The change works—Dunc and Damian battle it out under the hoop, but it's clear Dunc is better prepared than you.

After Charlie drains a three-pointer and Liu hits a pair of jump shots, it's clear the second half belongs to the Tigers. You quickly close the gap.

Deep into the fourth quarter, you find yourself down by two points. Saddiq brings the ball down the court. You line up to his right, behind the three-point line.

You break toward the hoop, getting your defender to bite. Then you step back again. You're wide open!

Saddiq quickly feeds you the ball.

> To fake the shot, turn to page 86.
> To take the shot, turn to page 92.

You pivot, get ready to shoot, and see the Viper defender racing back up to cover you. So instead of shooting, you pump-fake.

The defender bites, leaping up and trying to swat away a shot you don't take. Miles starts toward you. You can take the shot, but your eyes scan the floor, and you see Dunc and Charlie perform a perfect pick-and-roll.

Both of them are open. And there's not much time left on the clock.

>To pass the ball to Dunc, turn to page 93.
>To pass the ball to Charlie, turn to page 96.

Coach Willis is about to leave the locker room. You open your mouth to call out to him, but stop. Now is not the time to rock the boat. You can handle Damian Osgood. You just have to work harder at it.

This new bit of confidence seems to work. You hold the Viper center to a single shot as the third quarter ticks down. After Liu drops in a pair of jumpers and you make a three-pointer, the Tigers close the gap.

Turn the page.

You're happy the team is working together. But you still can't quite seem to catch up to the Vipers.

Damian hasn't given up his aggressive playing, either. Once, as you get the ball in the paint, he presses against you and says, "What are you gonna do, shrimp? Shoot over me? No way." When you try to put up the shot, Damian swats it away like a bug.

"Told ya," he says mockingly as the Vipers recover the ball.

The next time down the court, you try again. You push and shove and do your best to get open.

Saddiq passes the ball to Charlie, who sees you and bounces you the ball.

"You don't learn, do you?" Damian says.

You grasp the ball tightly, look out, and see Charlie is open.

To take the shot, go to page 89.
To pass the ball back to Charlie, turn to page 100.

Charlie is open, but you want to prove a point and show Damian you're better than he thinks. So instead of passing the ball back out, you throw your elbows up and pivot.

You extend your right arm with the ball, trying to hook the shot around Damian. He swats at the ball, striking you in the arm instead.

Tweep!

"Foul!" the ref calls. "Shooting two."

Your shot missed, so you go to the line for a pair of free throws. You drain the first one, closing the Vipers' lead to one.

"Great shot, bro!" Nick shouts. You hear him over the roar of the crowd.

Nick. The curse. You shake your head, trying to clear thoughts of the curse.

Turn the page.

You can't, though. As you put up the second free throw, you know it's off. It hits the rim and bounces into Brent's hands.

Seconds are left on the clock. And the Vipers are passing the ball skillfully to avoid a foul.

Just then, Miles passes to Brent, who bobbles it. The ball goes out-of-bounds!

"Tigers' ball!" the ref says.

Saddiq hurries down the court. He eyes the clock. Seconds remain. You post up, and Saddiq dishes you the ball. This is it. Brent is coming to double-team you, and Damian has his arm in your back.

But then you see that Liu is open.

> To pass the ball to Liu, turn to page 97.
> To take the shot, turn to page 98.

That rebound is all yours!

You dive for it. But so does Damian. He catches you off guard, and you both stumble to the floor.

Damian lands solidly on your right arm. Pain shoots from your elbow to your fingertips. You try to straighten your arm, but can't. "Ouch!" you hiss through your gritted teeth.

You stand and walk to the sideline. Coach Willis demands you go to the emergency room to have it examined. "But the game . . . ," you protest.

"You need an X-ray," he insists.

And so you leave the game with your parents. Your X-ray shows your arm isn't broken, but you aren't pleased. Charlie texted you. The Tigers lost.

THE END
To follow another path, turn to page 11.
To learn more about basketball, turn to page 103.

You have an open shot. No way you aren't taking it.

You turn toward the hoop, getting ready to shoot. The defender steps forward, throwing his arm up and forcing you to shoot early.

Swat!

He's able to knock away the three-pointer. The ball falls right into Miles's hands. The Viper point guard smiles smugly at you before dribbling up the court. He finds Damian on a fast break, and the center lays the ball in.

The Vipers have taken advantage of your error and extended their lead. The momentum shifts in their favor, and try as you might, the Tigers can't catch up. It's game over.

THE END

To follow another path, turn to page 11.
To learn more about basketball, turn to page 103.

Tick... tick... tick...

Time is running out. Dunc throws elbows in the paint, but you can see it in his eyes. He wants the ball.

You bounce a pass to him. He snatches the ball, dribbles, and turns. With one hand, he puts up the shot.

Damian swats at the ball, but misses and strikes Dunc's arm instead. The wobbly shot bounces off the backboard and falls in!

Tweep!

The ref points at Damian. "Foul! One free throw, Tigers!"

The game is tied up, and with Dunc's free throw, you'd take the lead for the first time.

Turn the page.

"You got this," you whisper to him as he goes to the line.

Dunc nods.

But his shot is off, striking the backboard and ricocheting off.

It's heading toward you and Damian. You leap up, snatching the ball from the center who dogged you earlier. In one swift motion, you put up a shot and drain it!

The Tigers have the lead, and there's no way you're going to give it up. The team bears down, playing aggressive, smart defense and holding the Vipers from scoring.

When the buzzer sounds, you've done it. You've successfully broken the curse!

THE END

To follow another path, turn to page 11.
To learn more about basketball, turn to page 103.

Charlie is ready for you. You dish the ball over to him. But he's not going to take the shot! Instead, he rockets the ball over to Saddiq, who passes to Liu, who finds Dunc open in the paint.

"Great teamwork!" Coach Willis calls out.

With all the fancy passing, the Vipers are confused. Dunc turns and fires the ball back to you. You're outside the three-point line. A made shot gives you the lead with seconds left.

You put up the shot. Nothing but net.

The crowd goes wild.

The Vipers try to bring the ball up, but there's not enough time. A half-court shot at the buzzer comes up short.

The Tigers have won their first championship!

THE END
To follow another path, turn to page 11.
To learn more about basketball, turn to page 103.

Damian's arm is pressed against your back. He's swatted away earlier shots, and you fear he'll do the same again.

You pass the ball out to Liu. You misjudge the angle, though, and Brent intercepts the pass! He quickly feeds the ball off to Miles, who hustles up the court. He easily slides in a layup.

You glance at the clock. Only a few seconds remain, and you're out of time-outs.

Saddiq inbounds the ball to you.

Three seconds ... two seconds ...

You're not even at half-court, but you have to launch a shot. As the buzzer sounds, the ball falls terribly short.

The Vipers win.

THE END
To follow another path, turn to page 11.
To learn more about basketball, turn to page 103.

The game is on the line. Seconds on the clock.

This is your time to shine—your time to show that there is no curse.

Damian's forearm is in your back. He's blocked earlier shots, but maybe you can trick him this time.

You spin, lowering your head and sliding the ball into your left hand. You start to bring the ball up, and Damian's long arms move to the ball.

Quickly, you shift it into your right hand and put up a hook shot that arcs around Damian and toward the hoop.

BZZZZZZTTTT!

Everyone in the crowd holds their breath. It's so quiet you could hear a pin drop. The ball descends toward the hoop. It hits the back of the rim, the front of the rim, bounces to the backboard... and rolls through the hoop!

The crowd screams. Coach Willis leaps into the air. Charlie and Dunc rush over and lift you into the air. "You did it!" Charlie shouts over the noise. "You've broken the curse!"

You look out and see your family in the crowd. They're cheering wildly. Nick gives you a thumbs-up.

This is a day you'll remember for the rest of your life.

THE END

To follow another path, turn to page 11.
To learn more about basketball, turn to page 103.

Damian's arm presses into your back. "You really gonna shoot against me again?" he snickers.

You've tried not to let him get into your head, but he has. You think of the last time Damian blocked your shot. The game is on the line now. You don't want that to happen again.

You pivot, throwing up your elbows and acting like you're going to shoot. Then, as Damian puts up his arms, you flip the ball behind your back and pass it to Charlie.

Charlie seems surprised to get the pass. Still, he handles it well. He shoots, but it bounces off the rim.

You and Damian both leap into the air for the rebound. The Viper center's elbow strikes you in the chest, knocking you back. But the ref didn't see it and doesn't call a foul.

Damian gets the ball and passes to Brent, who rockets it ahead to Miles. One jump shot later, their narrow lead is extended.

The Tigers keep trying, but you can't break the opposing team's momentum. As they celebrate their victory, you catch your brother's eye. Maybe next year, he mouths to you.

Maybe.

THE END

To follow another path, turn to page 11.
To learn more about basketball, turn to page 103.

CHAPTER 5
HOOP DREAMS

Basketball is a game almost anyone can play. It doesn't require a lot of equipment, other than a hoop and a ball. Basketball courts are found at parks and schools. Five players per team are on the court at one time. They include a center, who is usually the tallest player on the team and who tips the ball and scores under the net. The team also has two forwards who play offense and two guards playing defense.

Physical education teacher James Naismith invented basketball in 1891. Naismith was in charge of a group of rowdy boys at the YMCA in Springfield, Massachusetts. He needed an indoor activity to keep them occupied. Using a pair of peach crates nailed to a wall and a soccer ball, Naismith explained the "13 Basic Rules" of his new game.

These rules included no shouldering, striking, holding, pushing, or tripping. It wasn't long before Naismith's "basket ball"—initially two words instead of one—was a hit.

By 1893, basketball was being played in YMCA gyms around the country. In 1895, Clara Gregory Baer wrote a book of rules for women, and one year later, the first game of women's basketball was played. New rules were added, as well as changes to the game itself, such as dribbling. In 1894, Naismith asked the A. G. Spalding sports equipment company to design a leather ball just for the sport. Backboards were added in 1906, and the peach crates were exchanged for a circular metal rim and a net.

The sport moved from gyms to colleges around the United States. The first basketball league formed in the late 1800s. The first recorded college game took place in February 1895 in Minneapolis, Minnesota.

In 1936, basketball became an Olympic sport. The 23 national teams made basketball the largest Olympic team sports competition at the time.

In 1946, the United States and Canada founded the Basketball Association of America. There were originally 11 teams in the league. In 1949, the league's name changed to the National Basketball Association (NBA). It now includes 30 teams.

The Women's National Basketball Association (WNBA) formed in 1997. It has 12 teams.

Today, basketball athletes range in age from elementary school students to adults. College basketball is especially popular. Fans look forward to the annual National Collegiate Athletic Association (NCAA) tournament known as March Madness each year.

GLOSSARY

brick (BRIK)—a shot that goes off the rim or backboard and doesn't have a chance to go in the basket

fadeaway jump (FAY-duh-way JUMP)—a jump shot taken while jumping backward, away from the basket but still facing it

fast break (FAST BRAKE)—when a team attempts to move the ball up court and into scoring position as quickly as possible

full-court press (FULL-court PRESS)—a defense where the team pressures the opposing team the entire length of the court

key (KEE)—another name for the free-throw lane; the top of the key is the space where the free throw and three-point arcs meet

motion offense (MOH-shuhn aw-FENSS)—an offense where players move freely to open areas on the court

paint (PAYNT)—the area inside the lane lines from the baseline to the free-throw line

pick (PIK)—when a player sets a stationary block on an opposing player who is defending a teammate; this move is also called a screen

TEST YOUR BASKETBALL KNOWLEDGE

1. Which basketball player scored the most points in the NBA playoffs?
- A. George Mikan
- B. LeBron James
- C. Michael Jordan

2. How many players start each game per team?
- A. 4
- B. 5
- C. 11

3. Which of these teams is not a real NBA team?
- A. Miami Heat
- B. Anaheim Mighty Ducks
- C. Toronto Raptors

4. The player with the ball takes three steps without dribbling. Which violation occurred?

   A. carrying
   B. traveling
   C. overstepping

5. Who was the first NBA player to score 100 points in a single game?

   A. Wilt Chamberlain
   B. Kareem Abdul-Jabbar
   C. Stephen Curry

6. Which NBA team has the most championships?

   A. Los Angeles Lakers
   B. New York Knicks
   C. Boston Celtics

7. What violation occurs when a player uses both hands to bounce the ball?

   A. carrying
   B. double dribbling
   C. double handing

8. Which is not a starting position?
   A. power forward
   B. center
   C. power guard

9. As of 2020, which two WNBA teams are tied for the most championship titles?
   A. Los Angeles Sparks and Seattle Storm
   B. Detroit Shock and Phoenix Mercury
   C. Houston Comets and Minnesota Lynx

10. How many seconds are on a standard NBA shot clock?
   A. 10
   B. 24
   C. 40

Answers: 1. B; 2. B; 3. B; 4. B; 5. A; 6. C; 7. B; 8. C; 9. C; 10. B

DISCUSSION QUESTIONS

>>> Are you superstitious? If so, what are some things you do, in sports or otherwise, that show this?

>>> Imagine you are Nick, the main character's brother. You have lost to the Vipers before. How does it feel to watch your brother play against them?

>>> Discuss a moment in the game where the Tigers are victorious. Now discuss a scenario where they lose. How does each make you feel?

>>> Write about a time in which you played an important game. How was the experience? How did you and your team do?

AUTHOR BIOGRAPHY

Brandon Terrell is the author of numerous books and graphic novels, ranging from sports stories to spooky tales to mind-boggling mysteries. When not hunched over his laptop writing, Brandon enjoys watching movies and television, reading, cooking, and spending time with his wife and two children in Minnesota.

ILLUSTRATOR BIOGRAPHY

Fran Bueno was born and lives in Santiago de Compostela in Spain. Since he was a little kid, he has loved comic books. He was reading *El Jabato* at age eight, a comic book that his father always bought him, and in that exact moment he decided to become an artist. He studied at art school and will always be grateful to his parents for supporting him. His motivation is to do what he does best and enjoys most. He loves traveling with his wife and kids, being with friends, books, music, movies, and TV shows. Just a regular guy? He would agree.

CHECK OUT ALL 4 BOOKS IN THIS SERIES!

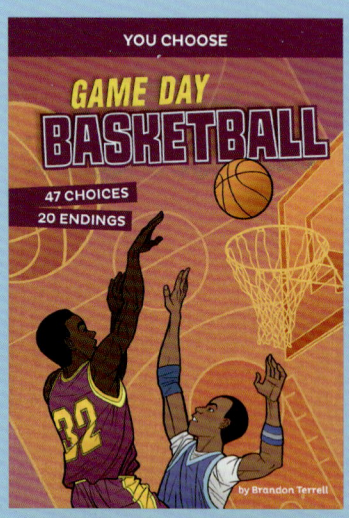

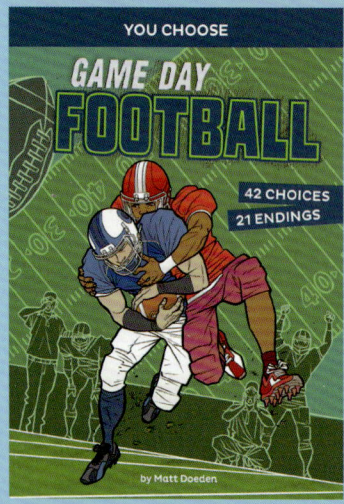

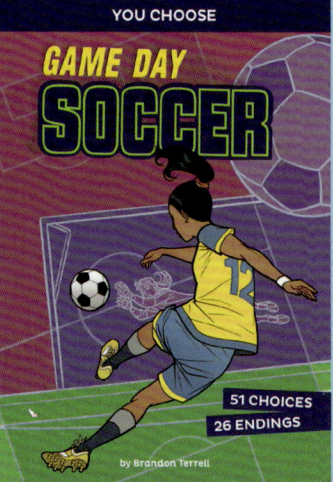

YOU CHOOSE

GAME DAY
BASEBALL

AN INTERACTIVE SPORTS STORY

BY ERIC BRAUN
ILLUSTRATED BY FRAN BUENO

CAPSTONE PRESS
a capstone imprint

You Choose Books are published by Capstone Press, an imprint of Capstone.
1710 Roe Crest Drive
North Mankato, Minnesota 56003
www.capstonepub.com

Copyright © 2021 by Capstone Press, a Capstone imprint. All rights reserved. No part of this publication may be reproduced in whole or in part, or stored in a retrieval system, or transmitted in any form or by any means, electronic, mechanical, photocopying, recording, or otherwise, without written permission of the publisher.

Library of Congress Cataloging-in-Publication Data
Names: Braun, Eric, 1971- author. | Bueno, Fran, illustrator.
Title: Game day baseball : an interactive sports story / by Eric Braun ; [illustrated by Fran Bueno].
Description: North Mankato, Minnesota : Capstone Press, [2021] | Series: You choose: Game day sports | Audience: Ages 8-11. | Audience: Grades 4-6. | Summary: It is the championship baseball game and the reader's choices can mean the difference between a triumphant victory and a heartbreaking loss.
Identifiers: LCCN 2020039524 (print) | LCCN 2020039525 (ebook) | ISBN 9781496696014 (hardcover) | ISBN 9781496697103 (paperback) | ISBN 9781977154255 (ebook pdf)
Subjects: LCSH: Plot-your-own stories. | CYAC: Baseball--Fiction. | Plot-your-own stories.
Classification: LCC PZ7.1.B751542 Gam 2021 (print) | LCC PZ7.1.B751542 (ebook) | DDC [Fic]--dc23
LC record available at https://lccn.loc.gov/2020039524
LC ebook record available at https://lccn.loc.gov/2020039525

Editorial Credits
Editor: Angie Kaelberer; Designer: Kayla Rossow; Media Researcher: Eric Gohl; Premedia Specialist: Katy LaVigne

Printed and bound in China. PO6238

TABLE OF CONTENTS

About Your Game 5

CHAPTER 1
A Comeback Season 7

CHAPTER 2
Flashing the Leather.................. 11

CHAPTER 3
The Ace and the Deuce 45

CHAPTER 4
The View from Behind the Plate 73

CHAPTER 5
America's National Pastime............ 103

Glossary 106
Test Your Baseball Knowledge 107
Discussion Questions 110
Author Biography 111
Illustrator Biography 111

ABOUT YOUR GAME

YOU are a baseball player with a history of practicing hard, playing hard, and making smart choices. You're known for your keen instincts and coming up big in tough situations. Your teammates look up to you, and your coach relies on you. But there's just one thing on your mind—can you lead your team to the tournament championship?

Chapter One sets the scene. Then you choose which path to read. Follow the directions at the bottom of the page as you read the stories. The decisions you make will change your outcome. After you finish one path, go back and read the others for new perspectives and more adventures.

CHAPTER 1
A COMEBACK SEASON

This baseball season has been a wild ride. Your team, the Rockets, started off slow. One of your best hitters missed the first couple of weeks with a sprained ankle and came back rusty. Everyone played as hard as ever, but the hits weren't dropping in and the pitching was cold. You went 4–6 through the first 10 games, and then you lost a heartbreaker to your biggest rival, the Railroaders, in extra innings. You were in fourth place and in danger of missing the Tri-City Tournament, the biggest event of the season.

Many of your teammates were feeling down after that Railroaders game. Even Coach Kowalski said, "Maybe this isn't our year."

Turn the page.

Coach calls you "the Bus" because you have a motormouth—and because sometimes you carry the whole team. You knew you had to say something to encourage your team members to keep trying.

"Come on, guys!" you pleaded. "Don't give up now. We're about to get hot—I can feel it!" Some of the guys nodded. But you could tell they weren't so sure.

Attitudes began to change when you won your next game. The game after that was an extra innings nail-biter, but this time your team came out on top. You followed that with another win. In fact, the Rockets reeled off five victories in a row and took 12 of the last 16 games.

The Tri-City Tournament is right around the corner, and you've made it in. After digging out of that early-season hole, the team believes anything is possible. But one thing is for sure—the Rockets can't afford another slump. That means you'll have to step up your game even more.

It's time to play ball!

To be a slick-fielding shortstop, using your highlight-reel defense to impact the game, turn to page 11.

To be a crafty pitcher, enduring high-stress pressure on the mound, turn to page 45.

To be a wise-but-tough catcher, managing the pitching game and hitting for power, turn to page 73.

CHAPTER 2
FLASHING THE LEATHER

Power hitters get the glory. Pitchers get the spotlight. But no team can be great without great defense. And no defensive position is more important than shortstop. That's where hard grounders come the hardest. That's where tough hops are the toughest. Where smoking line drives are the hottest.

That's where you play. Shortstop for the Rockets—it's where hits go to die, and everyone knows it.

The Rockets draw a tough matchup from a neighboring city in the first round. The Cyclones are known as big hitters. But the Rockets win a tight one, 3–2. In the second round, you blow out the Sun Dogs 8–1.

Turn the page.

Round three is against the Aggies, who score early and are nursing a 2–1 lead in the top of the seventh. With a runner on first and one out, the runner takes off. The pitch is a high fastball that the batter whiffs for strike three. Your catcher, Billy, pops to his feet and fires a perfect throw to you, covering second base. You pluck it just above the bag and slap the tag down—he's out! The play ends the inning, and the Rockets get ready to bat.

Everyone's feeling great. That is, everyone but you. The base runner at second came in hard and gashed your wrist with his spikes. You held on to the ball to get the out, but your wrist is bleeding badly. It's also throbbing with pain. You wrap it in a towel. The Rockets string together four hits and win the game on Billy's two-run double. Thankfully, you don't have to bat.

The win means you're going to the championship game. You celebrate with your teammates, but secretly you're worried. Your wrist is already swollen and stiff. It hurts to move it. You have just two days to heal. Should you tell Coach Kowalski? You don't want to sit out the big game.

> To hide the injury, turn to page 14.
> To tell Coach Kowalski, turn to page 16.

You keep the injury to yourself. No need to let anyone worry about it.

During the two days before the big game, you rest your wrist. No practicing. No exercise. You don't even play video games.

On game day, the wrist still aches, but it's a lot better. Your biggest worry is batting—will you be able to swing with authority?

It's a beautiful, hot summer day. The bleachers are full of family members, friends, and even a few kids from the neighborhood. Excitement is in the air.

Your opponent in this game is your old rival, the Railroaders. They blasted their way through the first three games of the tournament, scoring a total of 25 runs and allowing only six. They look loose and confident. They're not afraid of you, that's for sure.

They go three up, three down in the top of the first, and you don't have to make any plays. You feel a little relief. Then your team comes up to bat. You bat leadoff and slap an inside pitch down the left-field line for a double. The wrist hurts more, but the crowd's cheering helps you ignore the pain.

Unfortunately, the next three batters strike out, and you're stranded. You come up to bat again in the third inning with Billy on third and two outs. Coach gives you the sign to swing away, but your wrist is killing you. You are not sure if you can put a good swing on the ball. You do think you can lay down a good bunt against this pitcher.

To swing away as instructed, turn to page 18.
To bunt, turn to page 20.

You wait until the dugout has mostly cleared out, and you help Coach Kowalski bag up the bats and helmets. Before you can open your mouth, Coach glances over and notices your wrist. "Hey," he says, "what's with the towel?"

"I got spiked on that play at the bag," you say. "It really hurts."

You unwrap the towel and show him the gash—dried blood caked all over, two deep lines of shredded skin, and a big, swollen bruise. He asks you if it hurts, and you shake your head. It does hurt, but you don't want to admit it.

He gives you instructions to ice the wrist four times a day. He also says to take ibuprofen consistently to reduce the swelling and not to move it. "Rest and ice," he says. "Rest and ice."

You do as you're told. When game day rolls around, you feel a lot better. Not 100 percent, but pretty close. Your opponent in the championship game is the Railroaders, the team that beat you earlier in the season, and you can't wait.

Early in the game, with a runner on first and one out, you get a chance to test your wrist. A hot grounder is hit toward the hole. You dive, spear it on a short hop, and leap to your feet.

Your second baseman, Junior, covers the bag and awaits your throw. A double play would end the inning, but the runner heading toward second is almost there. You're not sure you can get him.

To take the sure out at first, turn to page 22.
To go for the double play, turn to page 25.

If Coach says swing away, then you have to swing away. That's your job. The next pitch is a fastball right down the middle. It's the kind of meatball you'd usually clobber. But because of the sore wrist, you're too slow. You pop it up in foul territory. The first baseman gets under it and makes the catch.

You're out.

In the top half of the fourth inning, the Railroaders' shortstop skims a grounder to your backhand side. You get there in time, but when you squeeze the ball, it pops out. Your wrist buzzes with pain.

Thankfully, the Railroaders don't score. When you get back to the dugout, Coach Kowalski calls you over to talk. "What's going on? You don't look right."

Maybe it's time to confess.

To tell Coach Kowalski about your bad wrist, turn to page 28.
To keep it secret, turn to page 30.

You know you can't get around on the fastball, not with this bad wrist. You might get in trouble for ignoring the sign, but if the bunt is a good one, Coach will forgive you.

The pitcher winds up. You pivot, lower the bat into the zone, and watch the ball all the way in.

Plink!

The ball kisses off the sweet part of the bat and rolls softly down the third-base line. It's a beauty! You drop the bat and run as hard as you can toward first. Out of the corner of your eye, you see the pitcher racing toward the ball. Ahead of you, the first baseman stretches to receive the throw. You make one last long stride toward the bag just as the first baseman makes the catch.

"He's out!"

In the dugout, the coach yells at you in front of everyone. "What was that? You got the swing away sign! We had two outs!"

"Sorry, Coach," you say. "I screwed up. I won't do it again." As you run onto the field, you just hope you'll get a chance to make up for it.

Your chance comes in the bottom of the seventh inning. The game is tied 1–1 when you come up to bat with one out. A kid they call Big Cheese is pitching. His cheese—his fastball—is the best in the league. Big Cheese keeps busting you inside with fastballs, and he's got you down 1 and 2.

You know the next pitch will be another fastball inside. You're not sure you can get to it with the bad wrist. But you might be able to get on base if you lean in just a bit and let it hit you.

To try to get hit by the pitch, turn to page 32.
To swing at it, turn to page 34.

It's better to get at least one out than risk not getting any. So you fire to first base. Easy out.

"Come on!" Junior says to you. "We had this guy." He slaps his glove against his thigh. The runner on second stands up and dusts off his pants.

"Just playing it safe," you tell Junior. Ever since you hurt your wrist, you've been playing cautiously. It's not your style.

The runner on second steals third and scores on a sacrifice fly. It's 0–1, Railroaders.

Back in the dugout, you try to fire up your teammates. "Let's get some hits!" But after two innings, it's still 0–1.

After three innings, it's still 0–1. The scoreless innings pile up. With each one that goes by, you worry a bit more.

It's still 0–1 in the bottom of the seventh—your last chance to score. Things look good when Billy leads off with a single. But Junior grounds into a double play. Two outs. Your pitcher, Max Carey, hits a line drive into center and stands on first base when you come up to bat. It's your big chance.

Adrenaline courses through you. You forget all about your bad wrist. Max takes a big lead off first. The pitcher winds up.

The pitch is over the plate.

You put a big swing on it.

Crack!

It feels good off the bat. The ball flies into deep right field. The right fielder runs back toward the fence. Max races around second, heading for third.

Turn the page.

The right fielder puts his glove up and catches it. You're out.

Game over.

The Rockets fall to the Railroaders by the score of 0–1. And that one run was made by the player you didn't double up in the first inning. You will be thinking about that all winter long.

THE END
To follow another path, turn to page 9.
To learn more about baseball, turn to page 103.

You grab the ball from your glove and quickly flip it to Junior, who steps across the bag and throws hard to first. The throw nips the batter by half a step—double play!

You and Junior exchange a high five as you jog off the field. Your experience and daring paid off.

It's a good thing, too, because nobody scores for almost the entire game. It's still 0–0 when the Rockets get their ups in the bottom of the seventh. Score here, and you win.

The Railroaders bring on a pitcher with a tough curveball. He gets the first two batters to strike out, but you crack a triple to left field.

Turn the page.

After hitting the triple, you stand on third base with the hot sun beating down as your first baseman, Bub, comes up to bat. Bub is an all-or-nothing hitter. He might hit it a mile, sending you to home easily. Or he might strike out and send the game to extra innings. On the first pitch, he swings wildly at a curveball in the dirt.

The pitcher isn't watching you closely, and you take a big lead, thinking that you might be able to make a steal. The count is 2–2, and you think he'll throw another curveball here. That's a slow pitch, and it will probably land in the dirt—hard for the catcher to handle.

To try to steal home and win the game, turn to page 36.
To let Bub try to hit you in, turn to page 38.

"I have to tell you something," you say. "My wrist is hurt—bad."

"When did this happen?" Coach asks.

"Last game," you say.

"And you're just telling me now?" Coach shakes his head. He takes you out of the game and puts José at shortstop. In his first inning in the field, José makes an error, and you feel even worse. The Railroaders get two runs, and your team is down 0–2 going into the seventh inning. But Billy knocks in one with a single, and the next hitter, Bub, walks. With two outs and two runners on base, José comes up to bat. The Rockets are down by just one run.

You hold your breath. There's a reason José is a backup—he's not as good as you. You're sure the Rockets are going to lose now, and it will be your fault.

Instead, José turns on a slider and hits into the left-center gap. Billy scores. Bub scores. Rockets win!

Your teammates run out onto the field. José is beaming with pride. You're happy for him and happy for the team. But part of you is jealous. You wish you'd been a part of it.

While the team is still celebrating, Coach comes up to you. "Take care of that wrist, OK?" he says. "We'll need you for fall ball. It's only a couple of weeks away."

"OK," you say. You almost forgot about fall ball. You can hardly wait.

THE END
To follow another path, turn to page 9.
To learn more about baseball, turn to page 103.

"I'm fine," you say. "Don't worry, Coach. We're gonna win this."

Two innings later, it's still tied 0–0 when a Railroaders batter gets a walk. During the next at bat, the runner at first takes off. Your catcher, Billy, makes a good throw to you. You snag it and lay the tag on the runner's ankle as he slides in.

The tag is in time, but the ball slips out of your glove when you make the tag. Safe.

You pick up the ball and walk it to the mound. "You all right?" Max asks you. You're famous for your good hands.

The runner scores on the next batter's double, putting the Railroaders up 0–1. Back in the dugout, Coach confronts you again. This time he sees your gashed and swollen wrist. He's furious that you weren't honest with him. "Selfish," he says, almost spitting the word.

José replaces you at shortstop and does OK, but a grounder gets past him that you are sure you would have had. All you can do is watch as the Railroaders tack on another run. The innings tick by, and their two-run lead holds up. They win the game.

At least you can play video games now. But that really doesn't make you feel any better about letting your team down. You won't make the same mistake next season.

THE END

To follow another path, turn to page 9.
To learn more about baseball, turn to page 103.

You're not sure if the sore wrist is the reason you're late on the fastball or if it's just worrying about the wrist that's making you hesitate. Or maybe Big Cheese is just too good. Whatever the case, your confidence isn't there.

So you make up your mind to take one for the team. As Big Cheese fires another smoking fastball inside, you lean in just a tiny bit. But the pitch was more inside than you thought. Instead of getting nicked, you get hit hard.

On the wrist.

Your bad wrist.

You drop the bat as pain shoots up your arm. You squeeze your eyes shut. Your knees go weak, but you start jogging toward first base.

When you get there, the base coach gives you a funny look. "You OK?" he asks you. "You're crying."

You realize he's right. Coach Kowalski comes out, takes one look at your face, and says, "You need to get that checked out."

Your mom takes you to the emergency room while the game continues without you. You don't know if the Rockets will win or lose, but you do know one thing. You're going to be more honest in the future.

THE END
To follow another path, turn to page 9.
To learn more about baseball, turn to page 103.

Let yourself get hit by a pitch? No way. You're going to take your cuts.

Big Cheese goes into his windup. You take a deep breath as you load up for a swing. The pitch comes whistling in and you slash at it. Contact!

A grounder skips just inside of first base and rolls toward the right fielder. Your wrist is throbbing with pain, but you ignore it. It's rally time, and you're safe at first base.

The next batter is Bennie, your team's best contact hitter. On a 1–1 count, Coach gives you the steal sign. You add an extra step to your lead. Big Cheese goes into his motion. You take off.

You safely slide into second. Bennie drives the next pitch over the infield into center. You dig hard for third. Coach wheels his arm to signal you to keep running. The catcher steps in front of the plate to receive the throw, but you slide in behind him. Safe!

Rockets win!

As your teammates rush out to celebrate with you, you forget all about your injured wrist. In fact, you never felt so good.

THE END

To follow another path, turn to page 9.
To learn more about baseball, turn to page 103.

You saw the way Bub flailed at the curveball. He's a big-time hitter, but you just don't think he's got this pitcher's number. It's time to take matters into your own hands.

The pitcher stands tall, both feet on the rubber, staring in at the catcher. You set your sights on his feet. As soon as that left foot lifts, you take off.

"He's going!" someone screams.

Dirt flies up behind your cleats with each step. The pitcher steps off the rubber and throws to the catcher. Bub steps out of the box, making room. You dive headfirst. Then you run your fingers across the plate just under the catcher's tag.

Safe!

You score the only run in a 1–0 pitchers' duel, carrying the Rockets to victory. In the end, your wrist didn't make much difference. It was your ice-cold confidence that locked up the win.

THE END

To follow another path, turn to page 9.
To learn more about baseball, turn to page 103.

You decide to play it safe and let Bub hit. Just as you predicted, the pitcher tosses another curveball. Unfortunately, Bub swings over it. Strike three.

The game goes to extra innings, and you sense your teammates are getting tense. Any mistake could cost you the game.

"Stay loose, boys!" yells Coach Kowalski, as if he read your mind.

Nobody scores in the eighth inning. The Railroaders seem as tense as the Rockets do. In the top of the tenth, you're playing in the field when the batter bloops a fly ball behind you. You run back, keeping your eye on the ball. You sense that your left fielder, Paco, is running in hard. But the crowd is yelling, Coach is yelling . . . it's hard to hear. Did Paco say "I got it?" You can't be sure.

> To hold up and let Paco catch the fly, turn to page 40.
> To handle it yourself, turn to page 42.

You don't want to have a collision, so you pull up.

The ball drops in for a hit, and the batter makes it to second base on the little bloop. "Where were you?" you yell at Paco as you pick up the ball.

"That was yours!" he yells back.

Two batters later, a ground ball scoots just under your glove near second base. The runner on second takes off—he rounds third base and scores. The next batter hits a triple, bringing the runner on first home. The next batter walks, and the batter after that hits another double, scoring two more.

By the time the Rockets come up to bat in the bottom of the tenth inning, you're down 0–5. Everyone is down in the dumps. You go three up, three down.

After the game, Paco gives you a sad fist bump. "My bad, man," he says.

"No," you say. "It was on me. I'm sorry."

THE END

To follow another path, turn to page 9.
To learn more about baseball, turn to page 103.

You keep running back, keep your eye on the ball, and reel in the fly. Paco jogs up and pats you on the back as you head for the dugout.

"Nice play!"

When you get to the dugout, the tone has changed. Instead of feeling tense, your teammates are excited. "Great catch!" someone says. "Now let's get some hits!"

The first batter is Paco, and he hits a single. The next batter grounds out, advancing Paco to second. Next up, Billy singles to right, but Paco has to stop at third because of a good throw from the right fielder.

It's first and third with two outs when you come up to bat. Feeling confident and pumped up, you swing at the first pitch you see. You rip it back up the middle, past the pitcher's outstretched glove, over second base, and into the outfield.

Paco scores the winning run!

THE END

To follow another path, turn to page 9.
To learn more about baseball, turn to page 103.

CHAPTER 3
THE ACE AND THE DEUCE

You're the ace. The number-one pitcher on your team. The guy who everyone wants on the mound when you just *have to* win.

So Coach Kowalski gives you the ball to start the team's first game of the tournament. It's single elimination, which means if you lose, you are out. No pressure.

The afternoon is hot with no wind and no clouds. Earlier in the day, the Railroaders defeated the Bears. Some of the Railroaders' players are in the stands to watch your game. You have a feeling that if you make it to the final game, it's going to be against them. They're the team to beat.

Turn the page.

After giving up a run in the first inning, you settle down, and the Rockets win 3–1. Two days later, your fellow pitcher Max Carey pitches game two, which the Rockets also win. The team's third pitcher, Bennie, starts the third game. This one is all offense, as neither pitcher does especially well. But in the end, the Rockets outslug the Cyclones for the win.

You've made it to the final game. The championship. And your guess was right. Your opponent is the Railroaders. Coach tabs you to start. You've faced this team before. They are a very good hitting team. They're dangerous.

Your job is to shut them down. You'll do it with your hard fastball and a cutter that darts toward the right batter's box. You also have a curveball that you can throw for strikes—a nasty weapon.

Unlike the last time you pitched, the weather feels like fall. It's cool. It's also a night game, adding extra chill to the air. Your hands are cold, and you can't get a good grip on the curveball. You're not getting strikes. You sandwich two walks around a strikeout. With runners on first and second, their cleanup hitter knocks a booming double. Both runners score.

Turn the page.

After the inning, your catcher, Billy, sits next to you on the bench. "What's up with the deuce?" That's what he calls the curveball—the sign for a curve is two fingers.

"Cold hands," you say.

"Shoot," Billy says. "Think we should scrap it?"

Without the curveball, you only have two pitches. It would be enough to beat many teams. But maybe not this one.

To scrap the curveball, go to page 49.
To keep trying it, turn to page 52.

The score is 0–2 as you take the mound in the top of the second. Relying only on your fastball and cutter, you get two strikeouts and a weak pop-up.

"You make it look easy," Billy says back in the dugout. You just smile—yeah, easy.

You pitch a scoreless third inning too. But the fourth opens with two straight hits. You get the next batter to chase the high cheese for strike three, the first out of the inning. But the batters are starting to catch up to your fastball. Not having to worry about the curve makes it easier for them.

Turn the page.

Next up is a big lefty named Sid. This guy has feasted on your cutter. So you don't give him any of those. Using all fastballs, you get to a full count, 3–2. He's sitting on that fastball now. He knows that's all you've got. If you throw another one, he'll be ready.

On the other hand, you've warmed up nicely now. Your grip feels strong. You think you might be able to throw that curveball now.

> To try to get a fastball past him, turn to page 54.
> To surprise him with the curveball, turn to page 56.

In the second inning, things start off badly again. You walk the first batter, with ball four coming on a curveball that drops in the dirt in front of the plate. You get a quick out on a fly to right field. Then the next batter singles. With runners at the corners, you strike out the Railroaders' pitcher with a cutter.

The next batter hits a dribbler off your curve. You hustle to make the play, but your throw to first is a hair late. He's safe, and the runner on third scores. That makes it 0–3.

Billy visits you on the mound. This game is about to get out of control. You think Billy is going to tell you no more curveballs. Instead, he says, "He barely made contact on that. It was a good pitch."

"Yeah," you agree.

"But the next batter is Jonathan." A tall, skinny player with freckles and long red hair is coming to bat. You've faced him many times. And for some reason, you can never strike him out.

"We can walk him," Billy says. "We have an open base. Put him on and face the next guy."

The next guy is their shortstop, a good fielder but not much of a hitter. Definitely an easier out.

To intentionally walk Jonathan, turn to page 58.
To pitch to him, turn to page 60.

This is no time to experiment with a curveball you *think* you can throw well. Sid wiggles his bat in anticipation. You reach back and throw your hardest fastball.

Sid unleashes a mighty swing and swats the ball deep into right-center field. It clangs off the fence as both the base runners score. Your heart sinks. It's 0–4. Runner on second, one out.

As you get ready to face the next batter, Sid starts dancing off second base. You look back. He's smiling at you. Daring you to throw him out. Your second baseman, Junior, shades a bit closer to the bag. He's ready for the throw.

You whip around and try to pick off the runner. But your throw is low and skips past Junior into center field. Sid advances easily to third base.

There's still only one out. You look over, and Sid is really smiling now. The next batter grounds out to first, but Sid scores on the play. It's now 0–5.

The Rockets get two runs back in the bottom of the fourth, and two more in the fifth. In the seventh inning, the Rockets are still down by one run when Sid steps up to bat again. He's wearing that big smile as if he just *knows* he's going to get a hit.

You could wipe that smile off his face. All you have to do is hit him with a fastball. He would get to take first base. But there are two outs and nobody else on base. You can get the next guy out.

To hit him, turn to page 63.
To pitch to him normally, turn to page 65.

Your curveball comes in spinning like a top and drops like a bowling ball. Sid, who was definitely expecting the fastball, swings right over it. The umpire calls it out: "Steee-rike three!"

Later, the Rockets grab a couple of runs, and going into the sixth inning, the game is tied at two. Your arm is getting tired, and you give up a hit but get two outs. That's when Sid comes up to bat again.

On a 3–0 count, Sid gets ahold of a fastball. The sound of the ball off his bat is like two bricks clapping together—*smack!*

You turn and watch it fly toward the fence. It's deep. Your right fielder, Jack, is racing back. Your heart feels like concrete in your chest. But Jack makes the catch on the run, right in front of the fence.

Nothing but a long, scary out.

Back in the dugout, some of the guys are putting on batting helmets and batting gloves when Coach Kowalski puts his hand on your shoulder. "How do you feel?" he asks.

You're tired, but you don't want to come out of the game. You want to be a part of this.

> To tell him you're fine, turn to page 66.
> To let him know you're tired, turn to page 68.

Walking Jonathan will be humiliating—everyone will think you're afraid of him. But it's the smart thing to do.

You walk him intentionally. As Jonathan takes his base, he looks at you. "Chicken, huh?"

Your face burns with embarrassment, but you funnel your anger into striking out the next batter on three straight pitches. Jonathan is left standing on first. The walk paid off.

After that, the Rockets start to hit. It's about time! You get two runs in the third and two in the sixth. Better yet, you have kept the Railroaders off the board since the second inning. Your curveball started biting, and they haven't been able to touch it. The seventh inning rolls around with the Rockets up 4–3. All you have to do is get three outs, and you win.

But the autumn wind has picked up, and it's getting hard to keep your hand warm. You get a strikeout but give up a hit and two walks. It's bases loaded with one out.

And who's coming up to bat? It's Jonathan, of course. And this time, you can't walk him. That would tie the game.

You have an excellent infield. If Jonathan hits a grounder, they may be able to turn a double play. That would end the game—and win it.

You could try to strike him out. If you can do that, you'd still need one more out. But the light-hitting shortstop is next.

> To try for the double play, turn to page 69.
> To go for the strikeout, turn to page 71.

You're not backing down from a challenge. "Let's get him," you say.

Billy nods. "Let's do it."

It starts off well. You get Jonathan to swing and miss on a curve, then you get a called strike on a chest-high fastball. Billy calls for a fastball next. You rock and fire. And Jonathan smacks it. Hard.

The runner on second scores easily, making it 0–4 Railroaders. You strike out the shortstop after that, and the Rockets score a run in their half of the inning. You go back out to pitch the third inning, and Billy was right about your curveball. It's back. You breeze through the third, fourth, and fifth innings.

The Rockets score two more, and you're losing 3–4 in the bottom of the seventh inning. Your last chance.

You come up with a runner on second base and lace a slider into the gap in right field. An easy double. The runner ahead of you scores. Tie game. Then, as you're approaching second, the center fielder bobbles the ball. You don't hesitate. You round second and dig for third. The center fielder makes a good throw, but you slide in under the tag.

Turn the page.

The next two batters strike out, but Billy comes up and singles up the middle. You trot home easily. Your aggressive playing led to you scoring the winning run. You can't wait to celebrate with your teammates.

THE END
To follow another path, turn to page 9.
To learn more about baseball, turn to page 103.

Sid really makes you mad. Always grinning when he beats you. It's time to send a message. So you wind up and throw your hardest fastball. It hits him in the ribs, and he collapses to the ground, the wind knocked out of him. His coach comes out to check on him. As you stand there watching, all your anger turns to guilt. What were you thinking? Hitting a batter? That's not who you are.

Sid finally gets up and jogs to first base. For once, he doesn't look at you.

Your focus has been rattled. You give up a walk and a hit, and Sid scores. Ugh. Now you're down by two runs. Coach Kowalski calls you into the dugout. He says, "Did you hit him on purpose?" When you don't answer, he shakes his head. He looks so disappointed.

Turn the page.

Coach brings in Bennie to pitch. He does OK, but the Rockets score only one in the bottom of the seventh. Your team loses by one.

After the game, when you line up to shake hands, every single Railroaders player pulls his hand back when you come by. They won't shake hands with you.

THE END
To follow another path, turn to page 9.
To learn more about baseball, turn to page 103.

Sure, Sid is frustrating. He's not a good sport. But if you hit him with a pitch, you could hurt him. That's not the kind of person you want to be.

So you toss a curveball for a called strike. He lets a low fastball go by for ball one. Then you burn him with another fastball. With the count at 1–2, you go back to the curveball. It comes in looking juicy, like it's right down the middle, but as he swings, it darts down and away. He misses. Strike three.

The Rockets tie the game 5–5 in the bottom of the seventh, and it goes to extra innings. Bennie pitches a perfect eighth inning for your team, and in the bottom half, the Railroaders bring a reliever of their own. It's Sid! The Rockets rally a run off him, and you get the winning hit. Now *that* feels good.

THE END
To follow another path, turn to page 9.
To learn more about baseball, turn to page 103.

"I feel great," you say. You must sound convincing, because he sends you out to pitch the seventh.

The first batter gets a hit on a fastball. You walk the next batter. You get a groundout, and the runners move up to second and third. Your arm feels like rubber. You walk the next batter.

Billy comes out to the mound. "I'm out of gas," you tell him. Coach brings in Bennie to relieve you, and you feel bad about the situation you've left him with—bases loaded, one out.

Bennie strikes out their center fielder, a good hitter. You relax a bit. But the next batter bloops a lucky single, and two runs score. The Rockets are down by two runs going into the bottom of the last inning. And they don't score any.

Your arm is going to be very sore tomorrow. It will be a painful reminder of how you cost your team two runs because you were too selfish to come out of the game.

THE END
To follow another path, turn to page 9.
To learn more about baseball, turn to page 103.

"I'm running out of steam," you admit.

Coach pats you on the back. "You pitched a great game."

The Rockets can't score in the bottom of the sixth, and Bennie goes out to pitch the top of the seventh. He's throwing so hard, you can hear Billy's catcher's mitt popping. The Railroaders can't touch him. You made the right choice.

The game stays tied until Jack smacks a home run in the bottom of the eighth. You and your teammates meet him as he crosses home plate and you celebrate your first championship!

THE END

To follow another path, turn to page 9.
To learn more about baseball, turn to page 103.

You decide to trust your teammates. Get the ground ball and let them twist the double play.

Jonathan digs in with his back foot. He looks out at you, waiting. You throw a fastball, low and inside. He lets it go. Your next fastball is just a touch higher, and he swings. Just like you planned, it's on the ground. It skips like a stone across a smooth lake, and your shortstop picks it. Quick and smooth, he fires hard to second base.

Junior, the second baseman, receives the throw and turns toward first. He rifles the ball across to Bub at first base, who reaches out to make the catch half a step before Jonathan gets to the bag.

"Yeah!" you yell. Double play. Game over.

Turn the page.

You line up and meet the Railroader players near home plate to shake. Jonathan grabs your hand and shakes it. "Good game," he says.

"You too," you reply.

"But you know what?" he adds. "I'll get you next time."

THE END

To follow another path, turn to page 9.
To learn more about baseball, turn to page 103.

Even if you get the ground ball, the double play isn't guaranteed. There's too much that can go wrong. Better to take care of this yourself. You're going for the strikeout.

You get ahead of the batter 1–2, and Billy calls for a curveball. You throw it, and Jonathan barely gets ahold of it. It flares toward deep short and deflects off the shortstop's glove. The runner on third scores, and the Railroaders tie it up.

You get out of the inning, but the Rockets don't score in the bottom of the seventh. The Railroaders end up winning in extra innings. You feel bad about the loss. But you went after Jonathan the right way. Sometimes people get lucky. You figure you can live with that.

THE END
To follow another path, turn to page 9.
To learn more about baseball, turn to page 103.

CHAPTER 4

THE VIEW FROM BEHIND THE PLATE

Catcher—that's the most important position in the game. At least that's your opinion.

It's the most fun too. Other fielders might get to handle the ball a few times per game, but you touch the ball on almost every pitch. You give the signs that tell the pitcher what to throw. You study batters for their weaknesses. You squat behind the plate and see the whole field. It's like you're a king looking over his kingdom.

The pitchers on the Rockets love pitching to you because you call a good game. You block all those pitches in the dirt. You don't just help them look good—you help them *be* good. Sometimes great.

Turn the page.

Of course, defense is only one half of the game. You also love the other half—hitting. You're not the best hitter on the team, but you have power.

Your team starts the Tri-City Tournament with some serious momentum. You roll through the first three rounds and make it to the final game. The championship. You'll be facing the Railroaders. They had the best record in the league, and if you asked them, they'd say they are the best team. They expect to win.

Of course, you didn't ask them. The only opinion that matters is yours and that of the other Rockets. Forget the regular season. The Rockets are the best, and you're ready to prove it.

For the big game, Coach Kowalski tabs Joey Basil to pitch—or, as you call him, Bazooka Joe. He has an arm like a cannon.

"Let's blow them away," you tell Joey.

In the first inning, Joey gets three quick outs. In the bottom of the inning, you come up to bat second. There's a runner on first and no outs. You smack a liner into right center and round first. As you look out, you see the right fielder picking up the ball deep in right field. You know he has a good arm, but you think you can stretch this into a double.

To go for second, turn to page 76.
To hold up at first, turn to page 78.

You turn the corner and hoof it for second. The second baseman straddles the bag and catches the throw from right field. You come in sliding, but he gets the tag down in time. You're out.

You jog off the field, where Coach Kowalski snaps at you. "Nobody out. First inning. We don't take silly chances in that situation."

You know he's right. You let your emotions get the best of you. You were too excited. "Sorry, Coach," you say. "I'll make it up."

The next few innings go by in a blur. Both pitchers are throwing well, and there isn't any scoring. You're calling a great game behind the plate, and Bazooka Joe hasn't even allowed a base hit.

You come up in the bottom of the fourth with a runner on third base and a chance to knock in the game's first run. The pitcher is pitching you very carefully. No more fat strikes—everything is off the plate. You work the count to three balls and no strikes.

The next pitch comes in high. You know it's ball four. But you also know that if you can get ahold of it, you'll hit it very far. Is it too high to hit?

To swing away, turn to page 80.
To take the walk, turn to page 82.

You take a wide turn at first but slow up. The throw comes in hard from the right fielder. You made a smart choice staying put—you would have been out.

Batting after you is your big first baseman, Bub. He cracks a hard grounder through the right side. Your teammate is thrown out at home. You advance to third. The next batter strikes out. Up next, Bazooka Joe grounds out. But you score the first run of the game on the play.

The Railroaders tie it at one in the top of the fifth. As your team bats in the bottom of the fifth, you watch the other team's pitcher closely. His name is Chance, and you've faced him before. But you notice something now that you never noticed before. Sometimes when he's standing in the set, about to pitch, he seems to move his hand around inside his glove. It looks as if he's trying to get the right grip before he throws. You watch him several pitches in a row. Each time he does it, he throws a curveball.

You're *almost* sure of it.

Do you tell your teammates? If they can know when the curveball is coming, it would help them a lot. But if you're wrong, it could really mess them up.

To tell someone about the tip, turn to page 85.
To keep it to yourself, turn to page 87.

You can't resist the high fastball. You know you can clobber it. So you swing away. And you make contact.

Unfortunately, you get just under it. A weak pop fly floats over the infield. The second baseman calls for it and catches it. The inning ends without a score.

In the top of the fifth, the Railroaders' speedy center fielder comes up to bat. He works a 3–1 count. He steps out of the box and looks down to his coach in the box by third base. The coach goes through a long set of signs. You've been watching him the entire game, and most of his signs are simple. Could the longer string of signs mean he's putting on some kind of special play?

Then you remember playing the Railroaders a few weeks ago. This center fielder bunted *twice* in that game. He's a good bunter. Is he going to bunt now?

If you call for a high fastball, you might be able to make him bunt it straight up into the air. Then you can catch it for an easy out. But if he doesn't go for it, it will be a walk.

> To call for the high fastball, turn to page 90.
> To call something else, turn to page 92.

You were taught not to swing at bad pitches. Even though you're hungry to get a hit here, you know your best bet is to take the ball.

The ump tells you to take your base, and you trot down the baseline to first. The next hitter gets a single and the runner on third scores. The Rockets take the lead, 1–0. Your patience paid off.

It's 1–1 when you lead off the bottom of the seventh. Once again, the pitcher is careful not to give you anything good to hit. You get another walk, representing the winning run as you stand on first base. The first-base coach gives you a fist bump. "That a way! Let's win this thing now."

Turn the page.

Sounds good to you. There are two outs, and your first baseman, Bub, digs into the batter's box. On a 2–2 count, he slices a liner into the right-field corner. You get a good jump and are rounding second base in a hurry. You're chugging toward third with a full head of steam. Coach Kowalski is coaching third base. At the last second, he puts up the stop sign. But you're going hard.

To stop at third, turn to page 94.
To ignore Coach's sign and go home, turn to page 96.

Your left fielder is in the hole, and you grab his shoulder. "Paco," you say. "See how he's rooting around in his glove right now?"

"Sure," Paco says.

"He's getting his curveball grip. Watch." Sure enough, the next pitch is a curveball. Bub swings and misses. You and Paco watch a couple more pitches. When Chance throws the fastball, he reaches into his glove and grabs the ball easily. When he throws the curve, he takes an extra couple of seconds to get a good grip.

When Paco goes up to bat, you tell the rest of the guys about the tip. You all watch as Paco lets two curves drop into the dirt for balls. When a fastball comes, he crushes it for a triple.

Turn the page.

The Rockets rally for three runs that inning. The Railroaders bring in a reliever, but by then it's too late. The Rockets hold on for the win.

"Great game," Coach says to you afterward. You got a couple of hits. You called a good game behind the plate. But your biggest contribution might have been just paying attention.

THE END
To follow another path, turn to page 9.
To learn more about baseball, turn to page 103.

You can't be sure, so you decide to keep it to yourself. The Rockets don't end up scoring that inning—and Paco, your left fielder, strikes out on a curveball that you definitely could tell was coming. But it's too late now, because the Railroaders tack on a run in the top of the sixth to take the lead. In the bottom of the inning, they bring in a new pitcher. He doesn't even throw a curveball.

In the top of the seventh, the Railroaders load the bases with two outs. Their biggest slugger, a first baseman named Sid, steps up to bat. If he gets a hit here, at least two runners will score. You are only down by one run now.

Turn the page.

Unfortunately, Bazooka Joe throws two curveballs outside. You put down the sign for a fastball—also called the big cheese—but Joe shakes you off. You do *not* want to go to 3 and 0 on him. So you walk out to talk to Joe.

"I'm not throwing him the cheese," Joe says when you get there. "He got two hits off my fastball today."

> To try to convince him to throw the fastball, turn to page 98.
>
> To let him throw curves, turn to page 101.

You're convinced this guy is going to bunt, so you put down a single finger—the sign for a fastball. Then you bounce your glove upward a couple of times to indicate you want it up. You settle your glove nice and high to receive the throw.

Bazooka Joe winds and fires. The batter squares around to bunt, just like you thought he would. The fastball comes in hot and high, just how you wanted it. But it's a little *too* high, and the batter pulls back his bat. Ball four.

He takes his base, and on Joe's very next pitch, he steals second. You try to throw him out, but you're not even close—he's too fast.

Joe strikes out the next batter, and there are two down. Maybe you'll get out of this. But the next batter hits a bloop single just over your shortstop's head. The runner on second motors around third and scores.

Nobody scores the rest of the game. You end up losing the championship 1–0, and you feel responsible. You see Joe walking to the parking lot after the game, and you catch up to him.

"You pitched a gem, Joe," you say. "I'm sorry about that run. It was my fault."

You'll get over it eventually. It just might take until next year's tournament, though.

THE END
To follow another path, turn to page 9.
To learn more about baseball, turn to page 103.

You don't want to risk the walk, so you call for another curveball, and Joe delivers a good one. The batter does square to bunt, but he fouls it into the plate.

On the next pitch, Joe blows him away with a fastball—inning over.

The score remains tied at zero through the seventh inning, and you go to extra innings. In the top of the eighth, the Railroaders score one. You come up to bat in the bottom half of the inning with two outs and a runner on second. Here's your chance to make up for all your mistakes. The out you made at second base. The walk you gave away by popping out on ball four.

Once again you work a 3–0 count, and you lick your lips. He's gotta come after you with a fastball down the middle—he needs a strike.

Here it comes. It's a little high again. You should let it go and take your base. But . . . *nah*.

You rip it deep into left field.

Really deep.

The left fielder is running back. He's at the fence. He's looking up.

He's *still* looking up.

He doesn't even lift his glove. That ball is gone.

Home run.

A *game-winning* home run, to be exact. A championship-winning home run!

THE END
To follow another path, turn to page 9.
To learn more about baseball, turn to page 103.

You stutter-step to a halt just past the bag and dash back to get safe. The throw comes in off-line, and the pitcher has to scramble toward the first-base line to get it.

You would have been safe at home. You're sure of it.

Your second baseman, Junior, grounds out to the pitcher, and the inning is over. You're going to extra innings.

José comes on to relieve Bazooka Joe. He's throwing hard, but he walks two batters. One of them comes around to score.

In the bottom of the eighth, you need a run to tie and two runs to win. The Railroaders bring in a relief pitcher. But unlike José, his control is good. He takes down three hitters in a row— groundout, strikeout, pop out.

You are standing in the on-deck circle with your bat when the game ends. You would have been next up. But you won't get your chance to make a difference. You should have taken the chance last inning, when you had one. Even so, you're proud of your team and how it played.

THE END
To follow another path, turn to page 9.
To learn more about baseball, turn to page 103.

You run through the sign and chug for home. The Railroaders' pitcher screams, "He's going home!" He sounds worried. You smile as you close in.

The pitcher receives the throw on one hop and turns toward home. The catcher moves on top of the plate with his glove out. Out of the corner of your eye, you see fans in the bleachers standing up to get a good view of the play at the plate.

The catcher gets the throw from the pitcher and turns to you. You fling yourself into a feetfirst slide. The catcher's glove comes down, fast and hard.

Your foot scrapes across the plate.

The tag comes down.

The catcher holds up his glove to the umpire to show him he still has the ball. But he was too late. You got in ahead of the tag. The fans in the bleachers are cheering even before the ump makes the call: "SAFE!"

THE END

To follow another path, turn to page 9.
To learn more about baseball, turn to page 103.

"Trust me," you say. "Let's challenge him."

Back behind the plate, you put down the sign for a fastball and set up inside. Sid is ready for it, but he pulls it foul. You call for another one in the same spot. Sid rips this one foul too. You get strike three on a heater high and outside.

Joe pumps his fist—that's a big out!

It seems to change the feeling of the game. Joe leads off for the Rockets in the bottom of the inning and slams a double. Paco bunts him to third.

The Railroaders' coach brings Sid over from first base to pitch. Not only is he a big, hard hitter, but he's also a hard thrower.

Turn the page.

Sid quickly strikes out Junior, and you step to the plate with the game on the line. A hit will win it.

And that's just what happens. You and your teammates hug and cheer as you celebrate the winning run!

THE END
To follow another path, turn to page 9.
To learn more about baseball, turn to page 103.

You don't want to walk in a run. But if your pitcher doesn't feel comfortable with the fastball, you don't want to argue.

You go back behind the plate. Joe throws the curve, and it's ball three. He throws another one for ball four. That walks in a run and increases the Railroaders' lead to two.

The next batter hits a soft grounder to first base, and Bub scoops it up and steps on the bag. You're out of the inning.

The Railroaders bring in a relief pitcher to finish the game. It's Sid. He throws hard and a little wild. With a walk, a stolen base, and a base hit, you manage to get one run back. But that's all you can do, and you end up losing the game by one. That walked-in run was the backbreaker.

THE END
To follow another path, turn to page 9.
To learn more about baseball, turn to page 103.

CHAPTER 5

AMERICA'S NATIONAL PASTIME

Baseball was the first professional sport to become popular in the United States and is nicknamed "America's National Pastime." Two nine-player teams play on a large field marked with four bases arranged in a diamond shape. Teams take turns hitting a pitched ball with a bat at home plate and then running around the bases in order to score a run. Players on the opposing team attempt to get the batters or base runners out, or taken out of play. Each team gets a turn batting during each of the nine innings, and the team with the most runs at the end of the game is the winner.

Baseball likely developed from two British games called rounders and cricket. In both games, players hit a hard ball with a stick or bat. Emigrants from Great Britain brought these and other games to the United States during the 1700s.

The modern game of baseball began in New York City. Members of men's social clubs such as the Gotham Club and the New York Knickerbockers wrote rules for the game. These rules established the diamond-shaped infield and three-strike rule. The first official "baseball" game was played in 1846, when the Knickerbocker Baseball Club played a team of cricket players.

In 1857, the Knickerbockers and 15 other New York clubs created the first organization to govern the sport. The National Association of Base Ball Players (NABBP) also established the first baseball championship. The NABBP created a professional category in 1869. By this time, baseball mostly resembled the game as it's played now.

In 1876, eight professional teams formed the National League. The American League formed in 1901, and Major League Baseball (MLB) was born. Two years later, champion teams from each league met in the first World Series.

In 2020, MLB included 30 teams—15 in each league. Today, thousands of fans attend games in huge stadiums. It's still America's national pastime.

GLOSSARY

bloop (BLOOP)—a softly hit fly ball that drops behind the infield for a hit

bunt (BUHNT)—when the batter gently taps the ball with the bat without swinging

cutter (KUH-tur)—a fastball that breaks toward the pitcher's glove-hand side as it reaches home plate

deuce (DOOSS)—a nickname for a curveball

double play (DUH-buhl PLAY)—when the defense gets two outs on the same play

dribbler (DRIH-blur)—a ball that is hit softly on the ground in the infield

heater (HEE-tur)—a nickname for a fastball

sacrifice fly (SAK-ruh-fisse FLYE)—when a batter hits a fly ball deep enough that a runner can advance a base after the ball is caught; the batter makes an out, "sacrificing" himself in order to help the runner

slider (SLY-duhr)—a fast pitch with a slight curve in the opposite direction of the throwing arm

tip (TIP)—when a pitcher accidentally gives away a clue about the pitch he or she is going to throw

triple (TRIP-uhl)—a hit that allows the batter to reach third base

TEST YOUR BASEBALL KNOWLEDGE

1. What does RBI stand for?
- **A.** Real Baseball Institute
- **B.** Runs batted in
- **C.** Runner bunted in

2. What's the name of the Major League Baseball Championship?
- **A.** MLB Cup
- **B.** World Cup
- **C.** World Series

3. "The Great Bambino" is a nickname for which baseball icon?
- **A.** Babe Ruth
- **B.** Joe DiMaggio
- **C.** Mike Trout

4. What base can you never steal?
- **A.** first base
- **B.** third base
- **C.** home

5. Which of the following is not a nickname for a curveball?
- **A.** the deuce
- **B.** Uncle Charlie
- **C.** the stink

6. How many players take the field on a baseball team?
- **A.** seven
- **B.** nine
- **C.** ten

7. What song do fans sing during the seventh-inning stretch?
- **A.** "Take Me Out to the Ballgame"
- **B.** "Closing Time"
- **C.** "Batter Up"

8. What is it called when two base runners steal a base on the same play?

- **A.** trick steal
- **B.** double steal
- **C.** stealy Dan

9. What do you call someone who can bat left-handed or right-handed?

- **A.** switch-hitter
- **B.** flip-hitter
- **C.** hot stick

10. What does it mean when a batter is "on deck"?

- **A.** He or she has been hitting really well.
- **B.** He or she is up to bat.
- **C.** He or she is next to bat.

Answers: 1. B 2. C 3. A 4. A 5. C 6. B 7. A 8. B 9. A 10. C

DISCUSSION QUESTIONS

>>> What is your favorite sport to play or to watch? Name three things that make it your favorite.

>>> In the book, the narrator has to make decisions about whether or not to stay in the game. What would you have done during these situations? Why?

>>> Many amateur and professional teams have one "star" player. Others have a group of average players who work together really well during the games. Which type of team do you think would be more successful? Why?

AUTHOR BIOGRAPHY

Eric Braun is the author of books on many awesome topics, including dinosaurs, astronauts, true daring escapes, and fractured fairy tales, but baseball is his true love. He never hit for much power, but he knew how to steal a base. Find more of his books at heyericbraun.com.

ILLUSTRATOR BIOGRAPHY

Fran Bueno was born and lives in Santiago de Compostela in Spain. Since he was a little kid, he has loved comic books. He was reading *El Jabato* at age eight, a comic book that his father always bought him, and in that exact moment he decided to become an artist. He studied at art school and will always be grateful to his parents for supporting him. His motivation is to do what he does best and enjoys most. He loves traveling with his wife and kids, being with friends, books, music, movies, and TV shows. Just a regular guy? He would agree.

CHECK OUT ALL 4 BOOKS IN THIS SERIES!

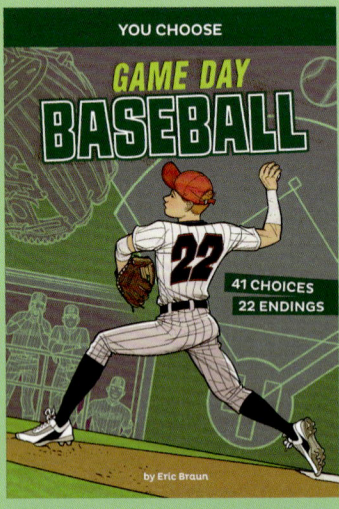
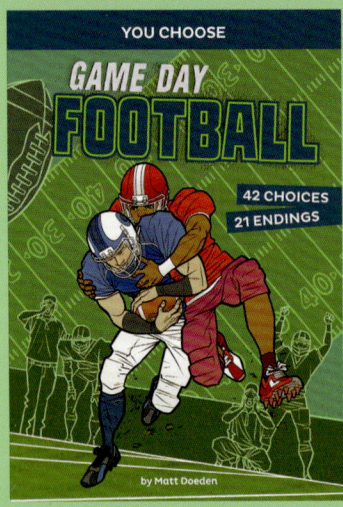
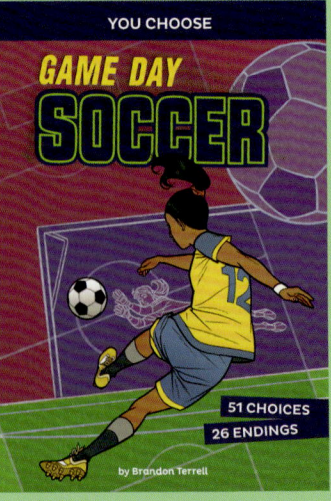